"You shouldn't

"Why not?" Angie star̶ but without fear.

Travis ground his teeth together. What was wrong with her? Any normal woman would have been trembling with fear right now. Didn't she know how vulnerable she was? "What am I going to do with you?" he asked.

"Do you have to do anything?" She brushed a lock of hair from his forehead and for a moment was reminded of all the warnings she'd heard about this man.

"Don't you have any sense of self-preservation?" There was almost a pleading note in his question.

"You make me sound like a gazelle trying to make friends with a tiger."

"That's not so far off," he muttered. But his head lowered towards hers, his fingers dug into her arms. "You shouldn't let me kiss you," he whispered, his mouth a heartbeat from hers.

"Who says I'm going to?"

"Your eyes say it for you."

Angel and the Bad Man

DALLAS SCHULZE

All the characters in this book have no existence outside the imagination
of the author, and have no relation whatsoever to anyone bearing the
same name or names. They are not even distantly inspired by any
individual known or unknown to the author, and all the incidents are
pure invention.

First published in Great Britain 1996
by Silhouette Books, Eton House, 18-24 Paradise Road,
Richmond, Surrey TW9 1SR

© Dallas Schulze 1992

Silhouette, Silhouette Sensation and Colophon are
Trade Marks of Harlequin Enterprises II B.V.

ISBN 0 373 16458 0

18-9606

Made and printed in Great Britain

Chapter One

He was a dark shadow on the twilit street.

From the toes of his worn black boots to the shaded visor of his helmet, he was dressed in unrelieved black. Even his hands were covered by black leather gloves.

If it hadn't been for the ear-rattling roar of the motorcycle he straddled, Angie might have thought him a figment of her imagination, conjured up by her urgent wish that someone would show up to help her out of her current predicament.

Of course, her thinking had been more along the lines of a *white* knight.

"Is there a problem here?" The helmet made his voice seem muffled and dark, just as the rest of him. The question was directed toward Angie but it was Billy Sikes who answered.

"Ain't nothin' here that's any of your business, man." The look he directed toward the man on the motorcycle was both warning and threat.

The stranger did not seem impressed. He turned his head to look from her to the five young toughs standing in front of her and then back to her.

"Is there a problem?" he asked again.

Angie wished he'd take off his helmet so that she could see his face. At the moment, she didn't know whether he was offering help or just a trip from the frying pan into the fire.

As if reading the uncertainty in her eyes, and guessing its cause, the stranger reached up to lift the helmet from his head. Shadow and light. The words sprang instantly to mind.

Shaggy blond hair brushed the collar of his leather jacket and the clear green of his eyes reflected the fading light. It was his eyes that decided it for her. Though she put his age at mid-thirties, his eyes were older, as if they'd seen too much. But behind the weariness was a touch of humor that appealed to her. There was something about them that made her feel warm inside. Despite the fact that he looked hardly less dangerous than the toughs facing her, she decided to take a chance on him.

"Actually I need to get to a pay phone," she said. "My car died."

"I don't see why that should be a problem. I can give you a lift."

"I'd appreciate that," Angie said gratefully.

But when she moved toward him, one of the toughs shifted to block her path. She stopped, her eyes meeting the teenager's with a calm she didn't feel. She'd hoped that, faced with something more threatening than a lone woman, they would give up the game but it didn't look as if that was going to be the case.

"Mind your own business, man," Billy told the stranger harshly. "This ain't nothin' to do with you. Just back off." Angie held her breath, wondering if the biker would abandon her to her fate. She couldn't blame him if he did. He probably hadn't counted on risking his life just to play Good Samaritan.

Moving without haste, the stranger swung his leg over the bike and stood up. He set the helmet on the bike's seat and turned to face Billy.

"I've never been very good at minding my own business," he said, sounding regretful.

Billy looked uneasy in the face of the older man's calm expression but he could hardly back down, not with his friends watching, waiting for him to show this intruder just whose turf he was on.

"Come on, Billy, let's split." That was Tony Aggretti, his dark eyes uneasy. In her position as nurse in the local clinic, Angie had helped his family more than once. He liked her and hadn't wanted to hassle her in the first place.

"We ain't splittin'," Billy snapped. "This jerk is the one who's splittin'. Maybe in a body bag." Angie caught her breath when the knife appeared in his hand, the blade gleaming in the twilight.

"You don't want to do this," the stranger said, seemingly indifferent to that length of cold steel.

"You're wrong. I'm going to enjoy this, man." With a harsh grin, Billy moved toward him. Flanking him were three of his friends. Only Tony hung back, looking upset.

Angie took a firmer hold on her purse. She wasn't going to stand by and see her would-be rescuer hurt without trying to help him. She started forward but Tony moved suddenly, catching her arms and pulling her back.

"You'll get hurt," he said sharply, holding her despite her efforts to pull away.

Angie was just about to deck him with her purse when it became obvious that the stranger didn't need her help. Billy feinted toward him with the knife, expecting his opponent to dodge back, putting him within reach of the youth who'd moved behind him. From the way they'd fanned out, it was obviously a move they'd used successfully before. But not this time.

The stranger didn't jump back to avoid the knife. Instead, he moved forward, stepping inside Billy's slashing thrust. His hand closed around Billy's wrist in an almost casual hold. With a cry of pain, Billy dropped the blade and the stranger released his wrist, bringing his hand up in a smashing blow to the face that dropped Billy in his tracks.

Even as Billy hit the ground, his opponent was moving, spinning to face the youth who was lunging at his back. In a move so graceful it was almost balletic, his feet left the ground, one leg kicking straight out. The worn leather boot caught his attacker just under the chin. The force of the blow lifted the younger man off his feet before he collapsed on the cracked pavement.

The stranger hit the ground in a crouch, his hands lifted, his fingers crooked, his eyes on the two remaining toughs. They hung back, looking from their fallen comrades to the man facing them. His calm gaze challenged them to continue the fight to the finish.

Angie held her breath, waiting to see what would happen. Tony still held her arm but the restraint was unnecessary. Obviously, her rescuer needed no help from her.

It must have been equally obvious to his two remaining opponents. They looked from him to the fallen bodies. He wasn't even breathing hard, yet Billy and Raul lay on the ground, unconscious. It must have occurred to them that he could have killed them without exerting much more effort. Both youths raised their hands in unison and took a hasty step back.

"Hey, man, we ain't lookin' for no trouble." The blatant lie would have been funny if the situation had been less tense. Even now, it was enough to cause the stranger's mouth to twist in a wry grin.

"My mistake," he said. Angie noticed that he didn't relax his stance. "Why don't you pick up your friends and get out of here?"

The two looked more interested in a quick departure than in carrying off their friends, but perhaps they thought the stranger might pursue them if they didn't do as he said. They moved to obey, keeping a wary eye on him.

"I'm sorry, Ms. Brady," Tony muttered. Angie hadn't even noticed when he released her arm. Now she looked at him, her blue eyes cool with displeasure.

"You should choose your friends more carefully."

He ducked his head, his eyes sliding away from hers. "They ain't so bad most of the time."

"They could get you killed one of these days," she said sharply. "Your mother depends on you, Tony. She loves you. What do you think it would do to her if you got yourself killed in some street fight?"

"Hey, Aggretti! You gonna stand there makin' time with the nurse or are you gonna give us a hand with Billy and Raul?"

Tony hesitated and Angie dared to hope that she'd gotten through to him. His eyes shifted from her to where his two companions were struggling to lift their unconscious friends. When he looked back to her, she knew she'd lost.

"They're my friends," he told her, his thin shoulders lifting in a shrug. He darted off before she could say anything more.

Angie watched the three boys gather up their fallen comrades. The stranger watched, too. Though his stance seemed relaxed, she didn't doubt that, at the slightest sign of trouble, there'd be more than two to be carried off. It wasn't until the would-be toughs had disappeared around a corner that he turned to her.

"You all right?"

"Yes. Thank you for coming to my rescue."

"You're welcome."

She waited but he didn't seem to have anything to add to the polite acknowledgement. He just stood there, watching her. She cleared her throat.

"You're not hurt, are you?"

"Are you offering to bandage my wounds, Nurse?" There was a wicked gleam in his eyes that made her cheeks warm, though he'd said nothing in the least suggestive. "They did call you a nurse, didn't they?"

"Yes," she said stiffly. "I work at the Fair Street Clinic. It's a couple of blocks from here."

"I know where it is."

"Oh. Good." Something about him made her think he probably *ought* to know where the clinic was. He looked like someone who might be needing its services.

"Not a good neighborhood for a woman walking alone," he commented. "Especially this close to dark."

"You're right." Angie followed his look, seeing the shabby businesses that lined the street, closed now, iron grills drawn across their fronts. "I thought I'd be okay because most people around here know me."

"They certainly did seem to know you," he agreed.

His mock solemn look drew a half smile from Angie. "I mean, they know I'm a nurse at the clinic. That means it's in their best interest to leave me alone."

"It didn't strike your young friends that way tonight," he pointed out.

"Billy Sikes is a very bad apple," she said, sighing. "The rest of them aren't so bad. But Billy's a real troublemaker. His mother died when he was twelve and he's been living on the streets ever since. He never really had a chance."

"My heart bleeds for him." His tone was dry and the look in his eyes said that he thought she was wasting her sympathy. Well, maybe she was but she couldn't help it. Billy had had so few chances to be anything but what he was.

The silence stretched again. Around them, the street had grown darker and Angie jumped when the streetlights came on. A few years ago, someone had done a study and discovered that pink lights were more soothing than the usual white. A well-intentioned city council had voted to replace the standard lights with the softer color, hoping that the gentler illumination would help curb the burgeoning crime rate in the area.

The effect on crime had been negligible. Angie couldn't speak for how a mugger might feel but the pallid pink lighting did nothing to make her rescuer look less tough. If anything, the soft glow only emphasized the hard look of him—and the interesting angles of his face, Angie admitted reluctantly. She cleared her throat.

"Well, thank you again," she said briskly. She hitched her purse strap higher on her shoulder, preparatory to moving on her way.

"I thought you needed a lift to a pay phone."

"It's not that far to walk."

"Far enough for you to get in trouble again. Hop on and I'll give you a lift."

She looked from him to the bike and tried to picture herself perched on the wide seat behind him, her arms wrapped around his waist. She was annoyed at how easily the image came to mind.

"That's okay. I really don't mind walking."

He leaned back against the bike and crossed his arms over his chest and looked at her with those clear green eyes that seemed to see too much.

"There are three alleys between here and the nearest pay phone," he said conversationally. "It's after dark and this is not the sort of neighborhood a woman should be alone in during the day, let alone at night."

"I'll be fine," she said, trying not to notice just how dark the street had gotten. And just what sort of business was he in that he knew exactly how many alleys there were between here and the phone? What sort of business encouraged a man to count alleys?

"If you won't let me give you a lift, I'm going to have to follow along behind you, pushing my bike. It's a big bike. Do you know how much work that's going to be?" His smile was teasing but it didn't hide his determination. He had no intention of leaving her alone.

Angie tried not to feel relieved. She wanted to be annoyed with him for not doing as she'd asked. But the truth was that she was no more anxious to be alone on the sadly misnamed Fair Street than he was to leave her there.

"I suppose, after all the effort you've already expended on my behalf, it would be ungrateful of me to force you to push your bike down the street," she said slowly.

"Extremely ungrateful," he agreed.

She moved toward the bike. "As long as you're going to give me a lift, would you mind taking me to the police station? It's only a couple of miles."

"The police station?" He straightened away from the bike, his eyes suddenly wary.

"Yes. My brother is a police officer, a detective," she added for emphasis. If he'd had any ideas beyond giving her a ride to the phone, hearing that she was a cop's sister would surely discourage them. "If the police station is a problem, you can just drop me at the pay phone," she said.

"It's no problem." The light made it difficult to be sure but there seemed to be a gleam of wry humor in his eyes, as if there was some joke only he could see. "At least if I take you to the station, I can be reasonably sure you're safe."

Angie's steps slowed. The closer she got, the larger and more intimidating her rescuer and his vehicle seemed. The pinkish glow of the street lamp reflected off the shiny black paint and gleaming chrome of the bike. She eyed it uneasily. Up close it was not quite so easy to picture herself astride it.

"It doesn't bite," he said, reading her doubt.

"Are you sure? It looks like it might have teeth."

"No. Cross my heart."

Angie decided to take his word for it. It was that or walk to a phone after all. And with the last of the sunlight reduced to a hint of red on the horizon, she had no desire to walk anywhere in this neighborhood. Given a choice between the unknown man who'd come to her aid or the well-known hazards of Fair Street, her choice seemed clear.

TRAVIS MORGAN watched the expressions flicker across her face and tried to remember the last time he'd seen anyone whose thoughts were so easy to read. Every emotion was revealed in those big blue eyes—just about the prettiest eyes he'd seen recently, he thought.

And the one pair of eyes he should stay clear of, he reminded himself. He'd heard one of the young punks call her Ms. Brady. Although Brady wasn't exactly a rare name, he was willing to bet that this particular Ms. Brady was Clay Brady's sister. Clay Brady, who just happened to be an officer on the Salem, California, police department. The same Clay Brady who'd probably punch him in the lip just for looking at his sister.

"Here. Put this on." She jumped, those wide-set eyes startled and wary as he moved toward her.

"I don't need that." Her protest was muffled as he set the black helmet on her head. It was too big for her and Travis had to bite back a grin as he looked at her. With those vaguely indignant eyes staring at him from under the raised visor, she looked like a little girl who'd been bullied into playing Darth Vader in the school play.

"I'm sure your brother, the detective, would be happier if you were wearing a helmet," he told her solemnly.

"I'm sure he'd be happier still if I weren't on a motorcycle at all."

"They're much safer than people think." Travis gestured toward the motorcycle. "Your chariot awaits."

A FEW MINUTES LATER, Angie decided that a chariot might have been a safer bet. When her companion straddled the bike and then held his hand out to her, it struck her suddenly that accepting a lift on a motorcycle was hardly the same as accepting a ride in a car. True, it was probably considerably more difficult to ravish someone on a motorcycle, but she didn't believe ravishment was on his agenda anyway. That still left the undeniable intimacy of sharing a motorcycle seat with him.

"Why don't they make motorcycles with a back seat?" she muttered.

"Because they wouldn't look as cool. Give me your hand and just swing your leg over."

Angie set her hand in his, feeling his fingers close over hers. The leather glove was softer and warmer than she'd expected. There was strength in his grip. Considering the ease with which he'd dispatched Billy Sikes and company, she'd been prepared for that strength. What she hadn't been prepared for was the odd little shiver that ran down her spine.

She wanted to attribute that shiver to the cool night air or nerves. But it was June in Southern California and the temperature didn't drop just because the sun had gone down. She might have been able to convince herself that it was nerves that had caused that odd feeling if her eyes hadn't immediately—revealingly—snapped to his.

And saw a quick awareness in his green gaze.

Their eyes held for only a moment, but it was enough to acknowledge the awareness between them. Angie shifted uneasily, tensing as if to draw back but his fingers tightened over her hand, drawing her closer instead.

"There's more room than it seems," he said, pretending not to realize the real reason for her hesitation. "It's a good thing you're wearing jeans. Motorcycles aren't made for skirts."

If there'd been anything remotely personal in his voice, Angie would have jerked her hand away and taken her chances with the familiar dangers of Fair Street. But there was nothing in his tone that even hinted at that brief moment of awareness.

Telling herself that perhaps she'd imagined it, Angie allowed him to draw her forward. Awkwardly she swung her leg over the bike. She settled into the seat with something less than grace and immediately discovered that there was no way to keep a polite distance from her companion. In fact, there was no way to keep any distance at all.

Uneasy at finding herself practically plastered against his back, she scooted back, only to clutch at his waist when he shifted the bike upright and booted up the kickstand.

"Hold on to me and lean when I lean," he ordered.

"I'm not sure—" The engine started with a roar that drowned out the rest of her sentence. She had only a moment to consider the possibility that a previously unknown thread of insanity might run in her family before the bike started with a jerk.

All thoughts of keeping a decorous distance from the man in front of her disappeared instantly. Angie clutched at his waist, pressing herself against his back as if the two of them were intimate friends. The bike roared down the street, pausing at the stop sign on the corner.

"Lean into the turn," he shouted to her over his shoulder. The reminder was unnecessary. Angie was holding him so tightly that she automatically imitated his every move.

They'd gone almost a mile before she dared to open her eyes to see where they were. After years of riding within the safe confines of a car, it was a shock to see the street rushing by so closely. But not an unpleasant shock, she admitted after a moment.

In fact, there was something rather exhilarating about it. Some of that feeling could have been inspired by the man in her arms. Her hold on him tightened as the bike leaned into a turn. If she were forced to be completely honest, she'd have to admit that she didn't feel nearly as wary of him as common sense demanded.

She felt a twinge of regret when the familiar brick police station came into sight. It occurred to her suddenly that he'd known exactly where it was. He hadn't had to ask directions. She pushed aside the thought that he might have a less than desirable reason to be acquainted with the location.

The bike came to a halt in front of the building. When he shut the engine off, the sudden silence was deafening. He pushed the kickstand down and it was only when he moved to get off the bike that Angie remembered to release her hold on his waist.

When she was standing on the pavement, she reached up to remove his helmet, shaking out her hair and giving it a self-conscious pat.

"Thanks for the ride," she said when he showed no signs of speaking.

"My pleasure." He swung his leg over the bike and sat down before taking the helmet from her. In the harsh light in front of the station his hair looked white-blond and cast concealing shadows across his face. "Do you have someone who can take care of your car?"

"Yes. My brother can take a look at it tomorrow." Angie almost regretted answering in the affirmative. If she'd said no, would he have offered to help?

"Oh, yeah. The detective." The curve of his mouth was oddly rueful. "Well, I'd best be on my way." He tugged the helmet on and eased the kickstand up before reaching for the starter.

"Wait." Angie took a step toward him as a sudden thought occurred to her. "I don't even know your name."

The bike was already moving but he glanced back at her.

"Just call me Galahad," he said, his eyes gleaming with laughter beneath the raised visor.

The bike roared off, leaving Angie staring after him.

Chapter Two

"You know, I never thought you'd come back." Bill Shearson leaned back in his seat and studied his companion across the table.

"Guess that's why you're not in the business of making predictions." Travis Morgan's grin was quick and sharp, and it stopped short of his eyes, which remained an icy green.

"Guess so." Shearson laughed and reached for his wine. "I sure thought you were going to stay out once you'd got clear."

"Yeah, well, plans change." Travis shifted restlessly, and glanced around the elegant restaurant. He would have preferred to meet somewhere less public. Didn't Bill know the place was probably crawling with cops, had been since Shearson's limo had pulled up outside?

Travis's mouth twisted ruefully as he reached for his wine. Nothing had changed. Bill undoubtedly knew exactly which of the patrons were actually undercover officers. Hell, he probably had several of them on his payroll. Bill never had been one to hide his light under a barrel. In the old days, Travis had told him more than once that a man in his line of work couldn't afford to be a public figure—it made him too vulnerable. Bill had only laughed and said that's what he hired people like Travis for—to keep him from being too vulnerable.

"So, you're interested in coming home, working for me again?"

Travis dragged his thoughts back to the moment.

"More or less. I can offer you something you want."

"I already have everything I need." Shearson's eyes were cool and watchful in his thin face.

"But you're not getting it at the price I can give you."

"Really?" Shearson turned his wineglass between his fingers, his eyes on the idle movement. "And where would you be getting such a good price?"

"If I told you that, you'd have no reason to deal with me, now would you?" Travis's grin was feral, his eyes ice-cold.

"We've known each other a long time, Travis. I'd think you'd have learned that you can trust me."

"I've known you long enough to know better." There was no malice in the words, only hard fact.

Anger flared in Shearson's eyes and for a moment, Travis thought his bluntness might have cost him the deal. But Shearson grinned suddenly.

"You always were too damned honest for your own good, Travis. I've missed that these past ten years."

"I bet you have." Travis took a quick sip of wine and met the other man's eyes. "Are you interested or not?"

"Maybe. But I didn't get where I am by being in a hurry." He studied Travis through narrowed eyes. "I'm surprised. You would never have anything to do with that end of the business. Why the change?"

"Ten years is a long time." Travis hunched his shoulders in a careless shrug. "Things change. So do people."

"I suppose they do."

Travis met the other man's eyes coolly, allowing no sign of the churning in his gut to show in his expression. This was the first step in getting what he wanted. He had to gain Shearson's trust, the way he'd had it ten years ago.

"An acquaintance saw you at the police station two days ago," Shearson said suddenly. Despite his casual tone, he was watching Travis carefully. "With a young lady."

"Yeah." Travis added nothing to the flat agreement. He wondered if the "acquaintance" was a cop on Shearson's payroll.

"A cop's sister, I believe?"

"So she said."

"Isn't that an odd choice of companions at this point in your life?"

"There were some punks hassling her. I helped her out." Travis shrugged to show how unimportant the incident had been.

"The knight errant?" Shearson raised one brow in mocking question.

"That's me, all right. Galahad." Travis had a sudden memory of saying the same thing to Angie just before he'd ridden off. Odd, how those big blue eyes had lingered in his mind. He shrugged off the memory. "Do you want what I have? Or do I look around for another buyer?"

"Where's your patience, Travis? You know I don't work like that. I'll need a little time to consider."

Time. A commodity Travis didn't want to spend. But something in Shearson's expression told him not to push. Not right now.

"Fine. I'll be in town for a while. I'm sure you know where to find me."

"I know where to find just about anything and any-one," Shearson said lightly.

Was there a veiled warning there? Travis wondered. He slid out of the booth after politely refusing Shearson's dinner invitation. This wasn't his kind of place. And he wasn't crazy about having dinner under the watchful eye of the local police, either. Shearson might enjoy being the center of attention but he was more comfortable in the shadows.

ANGIE GLANCED at the cloud-filled sky and then looked hopefully down the street. But there was no sign of her brother's car. What a day for Clay to be late. Of course, in all fairness, it wasn't his fault that a freak summer rainstorm had made an appearance. But it would have been nice if, just this once, he could have been on time.

She glanced over her shoulder at the clinic door. She could wait inside, out of the damp, but if she went back in Dr. Johnson was sure to seize the opportunity to ask her to help out—just for a few more minutes. Before she knew it, she'd find herself working until the clinic closed at seven-thirty. Hugh Johnson was a terrific doctor and she admired the dedication that led him to spend so many hours at the clinic but the man didn't understand the meaning of the words "time to go home."

Angie edged a little farther away from the glass door, preferring to take her chances with the unseasonable rain rather than risk being dragged back inside. She shifted her purse strap higher on her shoulder and peered down the street again. There was still no sign of Clay's car. A bright red 1957 T-Bird was hard to miss, especially in a neighborhood where the rusting hulks outnumbered the functioning vehicles.

A glance at her watch confirmed that Clay was overdue by a good half hour. If it were anyone but her older brother, she would have been worried. But this was Clay. Their father used to claim that being two weeks late at birth had set a precedent that Clay had never managed to overcome.

Any minute now, he'd show up, his hair disheveled, his expression harassed, full of apologies for keeping her waiting. If Angie had been a little less tired and a little less damp, the thought would have made her smile. As it was, it made her want to smack him over the head as soon as she saw him. She'd give him another ten minutes and then she was going to risk going back into the clinic to call a cab. One thing was certain, she wasn't going to walk to the nearest pay phone.

Not that last week's adventure hadn't had its interesting side, she thought with a smile. It wasn't every day that she was rescued by a man who said his name was Galahad. A man with eyes the color of pale emeralds. She'd half expected him to turn up at the clinic but she refused to admit to any feeling of disappointment when he hadn't. Maybe she imagined that spark of awareness that had seemed to flash between them. She frowned into the rain that was starting to drift down. No, she didn't think she'd imagined it. And she was almost positive that he'd felt it, too.

She sighed and pulled the edges of her light jacket closer together. It was just as well he hadn't shown up again. Considering the neighborhood and the look of him, he was probably something less than a respectable citizen. Respectable citizens generally didn't know how to defend themselves quite as well as he had.

It was a pity that none of the respectable men she knew had managed to spark more than the most anemic interest in her. And the first man in ages to send tingles up her spine had obviously forgotten her the minute he drove off.

ACTUALLY Travis hadn't forgotten her. She had, in fact, lingered in his thoughts a great deal more than he liked. It had required a considerable exercise of willpower to resist the urge to drop by the Fair Street Clinic to see if she looked as pretty in a uniform as she did in jeans.

Resist it he had, reminding himself that this was not the time to be getting involved with anyone, let alone a cop's sister. Even without Shearson's interest in their meeting, he didn't need to get involved with Clay Brady's sister. Not now. Not ever.

When he saw her standing in front of the worn brick building that housed the clinic, he reminded himself again of all the reasons it would be a mistake to pursue an acquaintance with Angie Brady. She was pressed against the wall, the narrow overhang of the roof offering scant shelter from the light drizzle.

Her car was probably still in the shop, he thought. Well, it wasn't his problem. It was also none of his business. Which didn't explain why, when he should have turned left, he found himself turning right into the clinic's tiny parking area.

Travis was still arguing with himself over the foolishness of the move while the Harley was bumping over the cracked pavement. He was mentally running through all the reasons why he should keep a healthy distance between himself and Angie Brady when he stopped the bike next to her and shut the engine off.

They stared at each other in the sudden silence. It wasn't possible but it seemed as if her eyes were even bigger and bluer than he'd remembered. And her hair was the same shining gold that he remembered seeing in pictures of angels. If ever there was someone who had no business consorting with angels, it was him. Especially such a tempting angel.

"Hi."

"Hello." Angie wondered if it was possible that she'd conjured him up out of her imagination just by thinking about him.

"Car still on the blink?" He reached up to lift the helmet from his head, propping it on one hip as he looked at her.

"The mechanic had to send for a part." She curled her fingers against the shocking urge to reach out and comb them through his hair, which had been flattened by the helmet.

"Is somebody picking you up?"

"My brother. But he's late."

"The detective? I'm shocked. What's the police department coming to?" His expression remained solemn but his eyes were smiling.

"I'm afraid the police department isn't to blame. Clay has been late for everything since birth. He was late for that, too."

There was a mutter of thunder and the rain increased. Angie glanced up at the sky and then looked back at the man in front of her. The gray atmosphere made his eyes seem almost emerald in contrast.

"You're getting wet," she pointed out.

"If it rains any harder, that roof isn't going to be enough to keep you dry."

She shrugged. "I can always go back inside."

Travis nodded. Of course she could go inside. It wasn't as if she was an orphan of the storm. *You've stopped and said hello. Now, put your helmet back on and be on your way.*

"Want a ride?" *Now, why on earth had he said that?*

"If it's not too much trouble." *Why don't you just throw yourself at him, Angie? I mean, don't give him a chance to change his mind or anything.*

"I just have to leave a message for my brother," she said.

"Sure. I'm not going anywhere." Travis hoped she didn't notice the touch of wry humor in his voice. Of course, he wasn't going anywhere. He was too stupid to do something that intelligent. Well, he'd just give her a lift home and then leave. No more contact. No harm done.

Angie was almost surprised to see him waiting when she stepped out of the clinic. Something in his expression had made her think that he half regretted his offer of a ride. She glanced up the street, not sure whether she hoped to see Clay's little red T-Bird or not. It was surely tempting fate to accept a ride from this man twice. She didn't even know his name, for heaven's sake.

"I don't know your name." She blurted it out as she stopped beside the bike. "I mean, I don't know your real name."

"You don't believe I'm Galahad?" he asked. "I'm crushed." But his eyes were laughing at her again and Angie found her uneasiness dissolving. It was simply impossible to be afraid of a man who could laugh without changing expression.

"I suppose your friends all call you Gal," she suggested, raising her brows.

"Not unless they want extensive dental work," he said, dryly. "Travis. Travis Morgan. At your service."

He tugged off his glove and offered his hand with an air of formality that was at odds with his faded jeans and black leather jacket.

"Angie Brady."

His fingers closed over hers. The first time he'd taken her hand, she'd felt a tingle of awareness, even through the leather of his glove. But it was nothing compared to the feel of his bare skin against hers. She'd never thought of a handshake as a particularly intimate act. But then she'd never shaken hands with anyone and felt as if she'd just touched a live electrical wire.

She kept her eyes on their linked hands, afraid of what she might see in his gaze. Afraid of what she might *not* see. How embarrassing if she was the only one to feel this odd connection when she touched him. But she didn't think that was the case, not if she could judge by the way his fingers lingered around hers. A slight breathless feeling remained when he released her hand.

Be careful, she cautioned herself. *It's one thing to be attracted to the man. But she couldn't forget that she knew almost nothing about him. And what she* did *know, hardly suggested that he was a model citizen.*

"Here." Travis lifted his helmet and set it on her head. "If you're going to make a habit of this, I'm going to have to get an extra helmet," he murmured, his hand brushing her chin as he threaded the strap through the rings that secured it.

Angie said nothing, hoping he couldn't somehow read her mind to discover that the idea of "making a habit of this" held more appeal than it should have.

"Okay, you know the drill." Travis held out his hand and edged forward on the seat, giving her room to swing her leg over. As soon as she was settled into place, he was reminded of all the reasons why he shouldn't have stopped in the first place.

Flicking the engine on, he tried not to think about the feel of her pressed so cozily against his back. Or about how nice her arms felt circling his waist. And he wanted to believe it was his imagination that made him think he could smell a delicate perfume drifting from her skin. The kind of scent that made a man think of cool linens and hot summer nights.

Glancing at the sky, Travis wondered if there was any chance for a little sleet. Maybe that would cool his libido. The rain didn't seem to be doing the trick.

Sleet in June was too much to ask for but by the time they'd reached the end of the block, the light rain had turned into a heavy shower. Before they'd gone two miles, Angie was soaked to the skin. The helmet kept her hair dry but it didn't do anything for the rest of her.

Not that she cared. The temperature might be unseasonably cool but she'd never felt warmer. *Shared body heat,* she told herself firmly. That's all it was. But that theory didn't account for the sort of tingle she felt where her hands were pressed against his stomach. She had the urge to curl her fingers into the leather of his jacket, to feel the skin and muscle beneath.

She flushed and tried to turn her thoughts in another more suitable, direction. Such as what she was going to fix for dinner. It was her turn to cook and the weather suggested something a little more warming than sandwiches. Spaghetti? Clay would enjoy that.

Just what did Travis look like without the bulky jacket? Without a shirt? Was he as leanly muscled as he felt? Was his chest smooth or covered in crisply curling hair?

How had she gotten from pasta to chest hair?

Angie was grateful that there was no one to see her reddened cheeks. Holding Travis around the waist seemed almost as dangerous as letting go and risking a fall from the speeding bike. She'd never, in all her twenty-five years, had such thoughts about a man she barely knew. Or about one she *did* know, for that matter.

Lightning cracked, followed by a low roll of thunder and Angie suddenly found herself grinning. There was something about the scene—the motorcycle, the man, even the rain—that made her feel like someone altogether different from the sane, steady woman she'd always considered herself to be. She felt wilder, freer, more exciting somehow. It was a rather nice change.

She tightened her hold on his waist and allowed herself to enjoy the wet ride.

Travis followed her shouted instructions, finally stopping the bike in front of a clapboard house that had been painted pale yellow. The house was old by Southern California standards—1920s, he guessed. With its wide front porch and crisp white trim, it would have looked perfectly at home in a small town somewhere in the Midwest.

It was exactly the kind of house he'd imagined Angie living in. Unpretentious but solid and sturdy. The kind of place where you expected to find grandparents rocking on the porch, watching their grandchildren play on the lawn.

But there were no grandparents in the Brady family. Travis had done his research and he knew the current generation was all there was. Just Brady and his sister. The same sister about whom he was having completely inappropriate thoughts. The kind of thoughts that could get him in trouble.

"Let me give you a hand." He reached back and took Angie's hand, trying not to notice the way her body slid against his as she eased off the bike.

Standing beside the motorcycle, Angie tugged off the helmet and shook her hair out. The rain had eased, at least for the moment, becoming little more than a light mist. A mist that caught all too invitingly in the pale gold of Angie's hair.

"Would you like a cup of coffee?"

"I doubt that your brother, the detective, would think it was a good idea."

"Clay would be the first to agree that a cup of coffee is the least I can offer." Travis hadn't seen Clay in years but he felt safe in predicting that he wasn't likely to agree to any such thing. "After all, you got soaked doing me a favor. Besides, he was the one who should have given me a ride home. So the offer should actually come from him."

Travis doubted that Brady would be inclined to offer him anything more than the shortest path to the door. Not that he could blame him. If it were his sister, he'd feel the same way. Brady didn't have anything to worry about, of course. He knew well enough that he had no business pursuing Angie, especially not at this point in his life.

"Coffee sounds pretty close to heaven right now," he heard himself saying. But not nearly as close as her smile.

He followed her up a cement walkway made uneven by time and the roots of the massive coast oak that dominated the front yard. She was wearing jeans again and he allowed his eyes to linger on the feminine sway of her hips. That enticing movement made it difficult to remember all the excellent reasons why he shouldn't even be talking to her, let alone having coffee with her.

Rather than going in the front door, Angie led him around the side of the house to another door. Somehow, it felt just right to step into a big country kitchen. It looked like the kind of house where the kitchen would be the real center of the home.

Angie pushed open the door and stepped onto the polished wooden floor. She shrugged out of her light jacket and then turned to see that Travis was still standing on the step.

"Come on in. Don't worry about getting water on the floor. The finish is so tough I don't think anything short of an atomic blast would hurt it. I'll put some water on to boil."

Travis hesitated another instant before stepping inside and shutting the windowed door behind him. After the cool dampness outside, the warmth of the room enveloped him as if it were a cozy blanket.

An old hunger washed over him, a hunger he'd thought long dead. When he was younger, before life knocked most of the dreams out of him, he'd fantasized about a room like this, a place that smelled of home. A place that felt warm and secure. The kind of place that practically demanded that you sink roots and build something worthwhile.

It had been a long time since he'd thought about those dreams, but they'd been niggling at the back of his mind ever since meeting Angie Brady. Which was another good reason to keep his distance from her.

"Nice house." He moved farther into the kitchen, stopping next to the oak island that sat in the middle of the room.

"My grandfather built it in 1925. Did most of the work himself." Angie's pride was obvious.

Travis leaned his hip against the island and watched as she moved around the kitchen, putting coffee in a filter and getting out mugs. It was a charmingly domestic scene. The sort he'd seen in movies but of which he'd never been a part.

When his parents were still alive, they'd spent most of their time traveling. He couldn't remember ever seeing his mother in a kitchen. He doubted if she'd have known what to do if she found herself in one. After their death in a car crash when he was twelve, he'd gone to live with his grandfather. It simply wasn't possible to picture Hiram Morgan in a scene of such cozy domesticity. Actually the word cozy and his grandfather seemed mutually exclusive.

"Have you been in Salem long?" Angie's question dragged Travis back to the present. He blinked, banishing the memory of his grandfather's large and chilly home.

"How do you know I haven't lived here all my life?" His tone was edgier than it should have been but he found himself wondering just how much she knew about him. Had she mentioned him to her brother? Had Clay somehow recognized the description?

"I've never seen you." If Angie noticed anything unusual in his voice, her expression didn't show it. She settled on a stool across the work island from him and fixed him with those wide blue eyes that made him think of angels and church choirs and, incongruously enough, candlelit bedrooms and slow kisses.

"Do you know everyone who lives in Salem?" A raised brow emphasized the question.

"No, but I don't think I could have missed you all these years." She flushed suddenly, realizing how her words sounded. Travis's grin told her that he hadn't missed the implication that she found him memorable. "The coffee must be almost ready," she announced briskly.

Travis waited while she poured two cups of coffee. He tugged off his gloves and placed them on the counter before taking a thick mug from her. If he noticed that she was careful to keep from brushing his fingers, she couldn't tell.

"Actually I used to live here. When I was a kid. But I left years ago. Haven't been back since." It was the truth, as far as it went. He cradled the mug between his palms and smiled at her.

"It's just that your motorcycle is so distinctive. I'm sure I'd have noticed it." *Right, Angie. As if you know a Harley Davidson from a Honda.* But Travis nodded as if willing to take her explanation at face value.

"Have you lived here all your life?"

"Except for the years I spent in college in San Diego. I suppose that seems strange these days. No one stays in the town where they were born."

"I think it sounds rather nice. It's good to have roots."

Was it her imagination or was there a trace of regret in his voice? As if he'd never had roots?

"Where are you from originally?" she asked, taking a sip of her coffee. It was a classic question in California, where almost everyone was originally from somewhere else.

"Nowhere, really. My parents traveled a lot. I was born in Africa."

"Africa?" She set her cup down and looked at him, forgetting her nervousness at this piece of information. "How long did you live there?"

"Less than a year. My earliest memories are of a station in the Australian outback. My father had decided to raise sheep. But we left before I turned five. From there, it was an ostrich farm in Wyoming. Or it might have been the botanical trek into the Himalayas. I'm not sure just what order they came in."

"It sounds fascinating."

"It had its moments," Travis admitted.

"Where else did you live?" she asked.

"It might be easier to remember where we *didn't* live. It wasn't as romantic as it sounds. A lot of the places were full of insects big enough to carry off a small animal. And the sanitation tended to be primitive, if there was any at all."

"But think of all the things you got to see," she protested. She set her elbow on the counter and leaned her chin in her palm. "And children never care about details like sanitation. They're usually quite content with the most disgusting arrangements."

"True. But I did occasionally think one of the bugs might just carry me off."

"You must have had some wonderful experiences," she said wistfully. Her eyes, as well as her words, invited him to continue talking.

Travis sipped his coffee, stalling for time. Actually he'd already told her more than most people who'd known him for years knew. There was something about those wide blue eyes that made it easy to forget the habits of a lifetime.

"It's not nearly as interesting as it sounds." He shrugged one shoulder, dismissing his peripatetic childhood. "I always thought it would be exciting to live in one place for more than a year."

"Exciting? I don't think I'd call it that but it has its good points." Angie accepted his change of subject, sensing his uneasiness in talking about himself.

"It can't be too dull or you wouldn't have stayed."

"It isn't dull." And it was showing signs of becoming downright interesting, she thought. "Is that why you came back? To put down roots?"

Roots? Travis doubted he was capable of having such a thing. Roots were for people like Angie, all sunshine and blue eyes.

"More or less," he said and asked another question before she could pursue the issue of why he'd returned to Salem.

She was telling him about her job in the clinic when the door behind him was abruptly pushed open, letting in a wave of cold air. She saw Travis tense and his right hand jerked toward the front of his jacket. It struck her suddenly that he was reaching for a weapon.

"Clay." She blurted out her brother's name, not sure if she was greeting him or warning Travis.

"Angie. What the hell were you doing? Leaving like that? Donna said you left with some guy on a motorcycle. I thought I was supposed to pick you up." Clay's scowling glance went from her to Travis's back.

"I thought you were, too," Angie said as she came around the work island. "After thirty minutes, I began to think you'd forgotten me. When I got an offer of a ride, I took it."

Her eyes met Travis's. His gaze seemed full of regret and an odd sort of acceptance. She had only an instant to wonder why before his expression became shuttered. Moving with deliberation, he set his coffee cup down and turned to face her brother.

"Clay, this is Travis Morgan. He's the man I told you about, the one who came to my rescue last week.

He seems to be making a habit of it...." Her voice trailed off when she realized that neither man was listening.

"What are you doing here?" Clay demanded.

"Having a cup of coffee." Travis waved one hand lazily in the direction of the empty mug.

"Get out." The flat command held a threatening undertone.

"Clay!" Angie's shocked protest might have been inaudible for all the attention it drew.

"Not very hospitable, Brady," Travis said.

Angie was almost as bewildered by his reaction as she was by her brother's hostility. Obviously the two of them knew each other. And Travis didn't seem at all surprised by Clay's attitude.

"Are you leaving or do I have to throw you out?" Clay asked.

"It might be interesting to see you try." Travis straightened away from the counter, a subtle tension in his stance. The change in him was abrupt and frightening. Gone was the man with the smile that started in his eyes. He looked cold and hard. And dangerous. Angie had a sudden image of the ease with which he'd taken care of Billy Sikes and his friends. She didn't know if he'd be able to handle her brother as easily but she had no desire to find out.

"Stop it!" She stepped between the two of them. "No one is going to throw anyone out." She threw her brother a fierce look. "*I* invited him here. And unless something has changed, this is still my home, too."

Clay opened his mouth to argue but Travis fore-stalled him. "Don't worry about it, Angel. It's not the first time I've been thrown out and it probably won't be the last."

He picked up his gloves from where he'd dropped them on the counter. Clay stepped back as Travis walked to the door. For a moment, the two men stood face-to-face. It seemed to Angie that something passed between them—some masculine understanding. It made her want to smack both of them.

Travis stopped and turned in the doorway. He was looking at Angie but she knew his words were at least partially directed at Clay.

"I'll be seeing you, Angel." A casual wave and he was gone.

There was a moment of silence and then Clay pushed the door shut. The quiet click as it settled into place was more eloquent than a slam. He turned to face her, his even features unusually hard.

"Would you like to tell me just what that was about?" Angie demanded before he could speak.

"Would you like to tell me what Morgan was doing in this house?"

"He was having coffee," she snapped. "Acting like a civilized human being, which is more than I can say for you." She snatched up the empty coffee cups and carried them to the sink, slamming them down with such force that they threatened to shatter against the thick porcelain.

"Since when do you go around inviting men like that home?" Clay demanded.

"Since 'men like that' save me from probable rape and give me rides home in the midst of a downpour." Angie flared, spinning to face him. "Since I'm a big girl and allowed to make my own decisions."

"You don't know him."

"I know that he acted like a perfect gentleman. *He* wasn't the one who stormed in here like...like...some sort of caveman. I've never been so embarrassed in all my life." *Or scared,* she added mentally. There'd been a moment when she'd thought the tense little scene was going to end in violence.

"I didn't mean to embarrass you," Clay said grudgingly.

"Well, you did a damn good job of it. What on earth was the matter with you?"

"I know Morgan."

"No kidding." She widened her eyes in mock surprise. "I'd never have guessed it. Where do you know him from?"

"We went to school together for a few years. Before he dropped out."

"Since when is being a high school dropout a crime?" she asked with heavy sarcasm.

"It's not that." Clay shrugged uneasily. "He had a bad reputation. A lot of girls. There were rumors that he was involved in some pretty ugly things after he left school."

"Rumors," she repeated flatly. "Was he arrested? Did he spend time in jail? Did you actually *see* him doing any of these 'ugly things'?"

"No," he admitted reluctantly.

"Then you don't actually *know* anything?"

"No." The admission was grudging.

"Then what's your problem?"

"He's just not a good person for you to know." He seemed to realize that, as explanations went, this one was more lame than most. "He's a bad man, Angie. In a lot of ways." His eyes met hers. "I don't want you to get hurt."

"That makes two of us." Her expression softened. There was no doubting his concern. His behavior had been unconscionable but she couldn't stay angry with him, not when he was looking at her with so much worry in his eyes.

"Travis has been nothing but kind to me, Clay. I like him." "Like" didn't quite describe the feelings he brought out in her but she wasn't going to go into that with her older brother.

"He's not a good person for you to like, sis. He's dangerous."

"I had a demonstration of that last week," she reminded him. "But I don't think he'd hurt me."

"Not physically. Maybe." It was obvious that only a sense of fair play forced Clay to concede that much.

"Well, it's a bit premature to be worrying about him hurting me in some other fashion. Besides, I probably won't even seen him again."

"Yeah. Probably." The prospect seemed to brighten his mood.

Angie turned back to the sink and twisted the water on. Staring out at the soggy lawn, she wondered if it was too much to hope that fate would throw Travis Morgan into her path a third time.

He was certainly different from anyone she'd ever known. Different and exciting. She'd never imagined herself attracted to a man like Travis—a man with such a dangerous edge. And no matter how much she wanted to dismiss Clay's concerns, she couldn't deny that Travis was dangerous.

It wasn't just the easy way he'd handled Billy Sikes and his gang last week. There was something more subtle than that, some feel about him that suggested he would be a very bad man to cross.

Angie felt a shiver run up her spine. It was not an entirely unpleasant sensation. Dangerous or not, she very much hoped that she hadn't seen the last of Travis Morgan.

Chapter Three

It seemed as if Fate was in a particularly uncooperative mood, Travis thought. Otherwise, why would she have put temptation before him so soon after he'd made up his mind to resist it?

Two days ago, when he'd left the Brady home, he'd decided that he was going to keep plenty of distance between himself and Ms. Angie Brady. The decision had little to do with her brother's hostility. The truth was, if he were her brother, he'd have felt much the same way. He just wasn't the sort of man who had any business hanging around a woman like Angie.

So, he'd had a short struggle with his conscience and decided to do the right thing and keep his distance. After all, how hard could it be? Salem wasn't a booming metropolis but it was hardly a village. In a town this size, it couldn't take much effort to avoid crossing paths with one pretty—okay, very pretty—nurse. Even one with the most beautiful blue eyes he'd ever seen.

But perhaps it was harder than it looked, he thought, slowing the Harley as he passed a supermarket, because getting out of her car and walking toward the store, was none other than the woman he'd promised himself to avoid. It was the first time he'd seen her in daylight without storm clouds softening the light. He couldn't help noticing that the bright sunshine turned her hair to pure gold.

Hardly aware of his actions, Travis turned the bike into the parking lot as Angie entered the store. It wasn't as if he was actually tracking her down, he told himself as he parked the bike. After all, a supermarket was a public place. It was hardly his fault that they happened to be shopping in the same store.

His conscience was still arguing with temptation as he pushed open the door and stepped into the store. It was a losing battle. Temptation won when he pulled a shopping cart out of the row and started through the store. He grabbed an item here and there, more or less at random. He might have to admit to himself that he'd come into the store in pursuit of Angie, but he didn't have to admit it to her. An empty cart would be a dead giveaway.

He swung around the end of the cereal aisle and stopped. Angie was studying a box of cereal, a small frown pleating her forehead. She was beautiful. She was wearing a soft dress in a blue that almost matched the color of her eyes. Her hair was caught at her nape

by a chunky white clip. She looked fresh and beautiful.

And like someone who should have nothing to do
with a man like himself.

He should just walk away here and now before she
saw him. He'd been right to decide to stay away from
her. Just as her brother had been right to tell him to get
out. If he had any sense of decency, he'd stay far
away—for her sake, even more than his own.

ANGIE GLANCED UP, startled, as another cart bumped
solidly against hers. She felt her heart give a similar
bump when she saw who the careless driver was. Travis
Morgan was leaning on the handle of the other cart,
grinning at her. Her fingers tightened on the cereal box,
denting the cardboard.

"Hi." She could only hope that her voice didn't
sound as breathless as she felt.

"Hi."

Maybe Clay was right. Maybe Travis was a bad man.
Certainly there had to be something not entirely good
about a man who could make a woman feel shaken and
breathless in the middle of a brightly lit supermarket.

"What are you doing here?" she asked and then
immediately wished she could recall the question. *What
did a person usually do in a supermarket?*

"Just picking up a few things."

"Me, too." Angie swallowed and made a conscious effort to drag her eyes away from his face.

"This is rather far from home for you, isn't it?" Travis commented.

"Yes." She stared at the brightly colored box in her hands, wondering what had happened to her brain. It didn't seem to be working very well. "Actually I'm picking up some things for a local family. The Aggrettis?" She glanced at Travis to see if the name meant anything to him, hoping it wouldn't. He frowned.

"Isn't there a Tony Aggretti who runs with that lout, Billy Sikes, the one who was hassling you?"

"Tony's not a bad kid," Angie said quickly. "He's just a little mixed up at the moment."

"So was Charles Manson," Travis said cynically. "Are you planning on taking these things to the kid's family?"

"Yes. Mrs. Aggretti can't leave the little ones."

"And I suppose they live in a lovely, safe neighborhood?" His lifted brows conveyed his doubts about that possibility.

"Actually they live in an apartment on Fifth Street." Angie lifted her chin, waiting for the argument he was undoubtedly about to give her. Fifth Street was lined with shabby buildings and even shabbier people. Muggings were so common that the victims generally didn't bother reporting them to the police.

"I was afraid of that." Travis gave her a look of exaggerated resignation. "I'll go with you."

Braced for him to try to talk her out of going, Angie was momentarily thrown off balance by his offer.

"You don't have to do that," she said automatically.

"Sure, I do. If I don't got, I'll spend the rest of my life feeling guilty for letting you go alone."

"The rest of your life?" Angie arched her brow doubtfully.

"Certainly." He gave her a wounded look that was so exaggerated, it made her laugh. It also made her give up the argument. It wasn't as if she had any real objection to his joining her.

THEY TOOK HER CAR, which she'd gotten back from the shop the day before. Travis folded his long legs into the passenger side of her compact without complaint. The little car put them practically shoulder to shoulder. Angie felt a warmth that had nothing to do with the fact that the car had been sitting in the sun.

Fifth Street was just as bad as she remembered. She wedged her car into a parking place between the rust-pitted hulk of a Ford and a shiny green Cadillac that had probably been paid for with drug money. Half a dozen young toughs lounged on the steps of nearby apartment buildings, eyeing the newcomers with sullen interest. "I hope you don't expect to see your tires when you come back out," Travis commented as he reached for the door handle.

"They won't bother my car," she said easily. "They know who I am, that I work at the clinic. They'll leave it alone."

"Right. Just like Sikes left you alone." The look he threw her spoke volumes.

"Billy Sikes is an exception. Most of the people around here know how important the clinic is. They may need us. No one wants to force us to close shop."

She slid out of the car and then leaned in to pull a sack of groceries out of the tiny back seat. After a moment, Travis followed suit. He wrapped his fist around the upper edge of the second bag and lifted it out. Let it seem like coincidence that he was keeping his right hand free. Angie might think that being a nurse gave her some sort of protection but he didn't share her confidence.

He watched her circle around the front of the car, her steps as cool and confident as if she was walking through a shopping mall. She nodded and smiled at a particularly tough-looking youth.

"How's your sister, Joseph?"

"She's doin' fine. Carrying a 4.0 average this year." His swarthy face broke into a boyish smile, and Travis revised his age estimate. Joseph couldn't be more than twenty-one or -two. Life had added years to his face.

"That's great. You tell her I said hello."

"I will, Miss Brady."

"*Miss Brady?*" Travis questioned as they entered the shabby apartment building. "He calls you Miss Brady?"

"His sister almost died as a result of a botched abortion. I stopped the hemorrhaging."

Travis followed her into the poorly lit stairwell. "And she's in college now?"

"In Los Angeles. She wants to be an architect."

Travis wondered how a girl raised in surroundings completely devoid of architectural inspiration should have such a dream.

"A scholarship?" he asked, trying not to wince as Angie started up a second flight of stairs.

"Partial. Joseph is picking up the slack."

"Drugs?" He felt her glance at him, as if trying to judge his feelings. He hitched the grocery sack into a better position and pretended to concentrate on the stairs.

"Not Joseph," she said emphatically. "There aren't many ways to make money around here but he's a hustler. He's doing the best he can with what life's handed him. Not like those damn parasites who bring drugs into neighborhoods like this, preying on those who live in poverty and despair."

Their arrival at the top of the stairs spared Travis having to come up with an answer. What could he have said? he wondered. Just what he needed—a woman on crusade against drugs. Damn, but he had enough complications in his life without adding Angie Brady to the list. As soon as she'd done her good deed and given the food to the Aggrettis, he was going to walk out of her life and *this* time, he was going to *stay* out.

THERE WAS definitely something wrong with the basic communications lines between his brain and his mouth, Travis thought. His brain was saying *keep your distance* and his mouth said *we could pick up some sandwiches and have lunch in the park.* The worst part of it was that he couldn't seem to regret the foolishness as much as he should.

There was something about Angie that put a dent in what had been—up until now—his excellent self-discipline. He'd come back to Salem for a purpose, one he couldn't afford to lose sight of. If there was one thing he knew how to do, it was stick to a purpose. He was nothing like his parents, always drifting from one scheme to another, never staying in one place long enough to finish what they'd started. He'd even been told a time or two that he was annoyingly single-minded.

So where did all that single-mindedness go when he was around Angie Brady?

"I haven't been here in ages. I'd forgotten how pretty it was."

Angie's remark drew Travis away from his brooding thoughts. He followed her gaze around the park. It *was* a pretty scene. It was early enough in summer that the foliage on the huge old sycamores was still fresh and green. There was still a shallow flow of water in the small stream that ran through the middle of the grassy park.

Later in the summer, the leaves would grow tired and dull and the stream would dry up. By late July, everything would be somnolent from the heat, dozing in the sun and waiting for the fall rains to start California's second cycle of growth.

"Hello? Did you fall asleep on me?" Angie's teasing question made him realize that he'd been staring at a particularly ancient sycamore. He shook off his uncharacteristically philosophical mood and turned to look at her.

"I was just thinking that I should have picked up a couple more of those brownies," he said easily.

"Not for me." Angie shook her head. "I couldn't eat another bite."

"Lightweight," he scoffed gently. He eased back until he was braced on his elbows and grinned at her. "You'd never win a pie eating contest."

"Fortunately for me, there aren't any coming up." Angie grinned at him.

He hadn't planned to ask her on a picnic, she thought. It was hard to say who'd been more surprised to hear the words coming out of his mouth. If he could have snatched them back, he would have and she knew it. A woman with any pride would have turned him down. Until recently, she would have said she had more than her fair share of pride. But there was something about Travis that made pride seem a bit less important than it had.

She shifted her position on the blanket until she could lean her back against a conveniently placed tree trunk and allowed her eyes to settle on the man in question. He was watching a mother playing with a toddler on the swing set at the other end of the park and it seemed safe enough to let her gaze linger on his profile.

She couldn't have said just what it was about him that made it so easy to ignore her common sense whenever he was around. Certainly he was an attractive man but she'd met other attractive men and her heart hadn't beat any faster. There was something else about him. He was so different from anyone else she'd ever known. There was an edge to him, a tension that drew her in a way she'd never experienced.

But it wasn't just his green eyes or the air of danger that attracted her. It was something a little harder to dismiss.

"I saw you slip money to Mrs. Aggretti," she told him. "That was very nice of you."

"It was nothing." He sat up, hunching his shoulders uneasily under the soft cotton of his shirt. "Just a few bucks."

"Well, it's more than she had."

"Where's her husband?"

"He left her just before the baby was born. Ran off with a waitress from the topless bar where he was working. No one has heard from him since."

"He ought to be shot," Travis growled.

"I'll provide the bullets," she said in agreement. She leaned forward, drawing her knees up under her full skirt and wrapping her arms around them. The problems of the Aggretti family really touched him. It didn't fit with the leather jacketed, tough guy image he projected. And it didn't fit with what Clay had said about him.

"Clay told me I should stay away from you." She hadn't realized what she was going to say until she heard the words coming out. She watched Travis, waiting for some reaction. Other than a slight deepening of the lines around his mouth, there was nothing to be seen.

"He's probably right," he said after a moment. He glanced at her, his eyes expressionless.

"Why?" Angie frowned, annoyed by his casual response.

"Didn't he tell you why?" He reached for the leather jacket he'd discarded earlier. Angie had the strange thought that he was reaching for armor of a sort, as if the tough looking jacket shielded him from more than just a cool breeze. She caught hold of it, preventing him from putting it on.

"He said you were a bad man for a woman to know. He seemed to think you'd hurt me. I think he's wrong," she added boldly, only just then making up her mind.

Reluctantly Travis lifted his eyes to her face. Hurt her? Not willingly. But that didn't mean she wouldn't get hurt anyway. The nature of his business was such that anyone who cared about him was at risk.

"Clay said that the two of you were in school together." Angie waited for his response.

"I wouldn't put it quite that way," he said, his mouth twisting dryly. "We went to the same school for a couple of years but we hardly ran in the same crowd." He shrugged. "It was a long time ago."

"Are you wanted by the police?" The stark question drew a grim laugh from him.

"I'm not dodging arrest warrants, if that's what you mean."

"But the police are interested in you?"

"It's hard to say who they'll take an interest in," he said evasively. His eyes dropped to where her fingers were curled over the sleeve of his jacket. Her nails were cut short and unpolished. Her hands were small but there was strength in them. They were the sort of hands a man could trust. At least they would be if he could afford to trust anyone.

"You should listen to your brother, Angel." He released his hold on the jacket to take her hand in his. Running his thumb over the back of her hand, he looked for the right words to make her see how impossible a relationship between them would be.

"I've never listened to Clay before," she said lightly. "I don't see any reason to break a family tradition now."

"Some traditions are meant to be broken." But her words drew a reluctant smile from him. There was something very appealing about her determined optimism. He suspected if she were faced with a handful of lemons, Angie would do her damnedest to make lemonade. And probably succeed. But it would take more than a scoopful of sugar to sweeten his life.

"I don't think you're as bad as you'd like people to believe," she said. Tilting her head consideringly, she studied him. Travis shifted uneasily under that interested blue gaze. It made him feel like an unusual species of insect being studied beneath a microscope.

"Maybe I'm a lot worse than you think," he suggested, only half joking.

"I don't think so. I think you put up that bad boy front to keep people at a distance."

Travis moved so quickly that she had time for only a startled gasp before she found herself lying flat on her back in the cool grass. Travis's wide shoulders loomed over her, blocking out the leafy canopy above them.

"You shouldn't be so trusting," he snapped.

"Why not?" She stared up at him, her eyes startled but without fear.

Travis ground his teeth together. What was wrong with her? Any normal woman would have been trembling with fear right now. Didn't she know how vulnerable she was? How easily he could hurt her? She barely knew him. She had no business looking up at him with those big blue eyes as if she hadn't a fear in the world. His hands gentled on her arms.

"What am I going to do with you?"

"Do you have to do anything?" She reached up to brush a lock of dark gold hair from his forehead, something she'd been tempted to do almost from the moment they met.

His quick move had startled her more than she'd let on. For a moment, she'd been reminded of his capacity for violence. But it had only been for a moment. Somewhere inside her there was a deep certainty that he wouldn't hurt her. It wasn't based on logic, and it certainly wasn't based on extensive experience with the man. Logic and experience both suggested that she heed her brother's warning and keep a safe distance.

"Don't you have any sense of self-preservation?" There was an almost pleading note in the question.

"You make me sound like a gazelle trying to make friends with a tiger."

"That's not so far off," he muttered. But his eyes drifted to where the dappled sunlight turned her hair to patchy gold and convincing her to stay away from him suddenly didn't seem quite so important. It seemed more important that, even in shadow, her eyes were a clear and shining blue.

He lowered his head toward hers, seeing awareness flare in her eyes. Her fingers dug into the muscles of his upper arms, not in protest, but in approval.

"You shouldn't let me kiss you," he told her, his mouth a heartbeat away from hers.

"Who says I'm going to?" she whispered breathlessly.

"Your eyes say it for you."

Her mouth was as soft as he'd imagined it to be. Soft and warm and welcoming. Her lips carried the taste of the orange soda she'd had with lunch. Travis hadn't realized how good the sweet drink tasted until he drank it from Angie's lips. It was possible that heaven tasted like Orange Crush.

Or maybe heaven just tasted like Angie Brady, he decided, tilting his head to deepen the kiss. His tongue feathered over her lower lip and he felt more than heard her soft sigh of surrender. Her hands tightened on his arms as her mouth opened for him. Paradise beckoned. And he hadn't the strength to turn his back on it.

"Morgan." The voice shattered the fragile moment.

Angie felt the impact of the single word strike Travis. For a split second, he remained frozen and then his head came up, his eyes meeting hers for an instant before he rolled away from her. The move brought him to his feet, as graceful as a hunting cat.

Dazed by the abrupt change of mood, Angie sat up. She pushed her hair back from her face and looked at the two men who'd interrupted them. They were standing a few feet away, their backs to the sun, making them little more than bulky silhouettes to her.

"We got a message for you." It was the one on the left who spoke. Though the words were innocuous enough, there was menace in his tone.

"You could have sent a card," Travis said lightly.

"It's the kind of message better delivered in person," the other man told him. Angie was glad that the light prevented her from seeing his face. She had the feeling that he was smiling and she didn't think it was a particularly pleasant expression.

"Travis?" She scrambled to her feet and edged closer to him, looking for some reassurance in his eyes. It was odd how the temperature had suddenly dropped. The park that had been so pleasantly quiet a few minutes ago now seemed ominously isolated.

"Perhaps your lady friend would like to go home," the stranger suggested politely.

"I'm not going anywhere," Angie snapped, taking hold of Travis's sleeve. Whatever they had in mind, surely they wouldn't do anything as long as she was there.

"Go home, Angie." Travis lifted her hand from his arm. "Go home."

"Come with me." She lowered her voice to a whisper, looking at him with pleading eyes.

"I have business to take care of," he said, shaking his head.

"I don't think they brought their briefcases," she muttered, casting an uneasy look at the two men.

His mouth twisted in a half smile but the humor didn't reach his eyes. "Go on. It's okay."

Angie wanted to argue but she couldn't fight the command in his eyes. He looked every inch the man Clay had warned her against. The cold in his eyes sent a shiver up her spine, even though the look wasn't intended for her.

She bent down and scooped up the old blanket they'd used for their picnic and bundled it over her arm. She cast a last, uneasy look at Travis, wishing he'd leave with her, and at the same time, half frightened by the abrupt change in his expression.

Turning away, she hurried toward the car, trying not to consider that Clay might have been right. Maybe Travis Morgan *was* more than she could handle.

Chapter Four

She really didn't know Travis Morgan well enough to be worried about him, Angie reminded herself as she squinted at the faded numbers on the crumbling curbs. Their acquaintance had been eventful but brief. She knew little more about him than his name and that his parents had traveled a lot when he was young.

So the concern she felt wasn't a really *personal* kind of thing, she assured herself for at least the tenth time. She was a nurse. A certain *impersonal* concern was a natural part of her job. She just wanted to make sure he was all right. It was practically her duty, she reminded herself.

It had been three days since she and Travis had shared their picnic. Three days since she'd left him alone with those two large and distinctly hostile-looking men in dark suits.

She felt as if her life had changed in some subtle way—as if she'd changed since she met him. What was she doing? she asked herself. She was practically chasing after a man she hardly knew. But she didn't turn the car around.

Angie edged her little compact next to the curb and got out. Standing beside the car, she shaded her eyes with her hand and studied the shabby little house before her. There was nothing to distinguish it from the houses around it. The paint was peeling and the roof had an uneasy sag in the middle. The old wooden window frames had enough coats of paint to make opening them an unlikely prospect. The lawn still showed traces of green but by midsummer it would be the same tawny color as its neighbors.

The only incongruous note in the whole picture of age and decay was the solid new door on the garage. Angie smiled when she saw it. Typical of a man to add a new garage door to protect his motorcycle and let the house continue to slide into ruin. She hoped the motorcycle was all that door was protecting.

She frowned as she turned back to the car to get her tote bag. It wouldn't do to forget how little she knew about Travis. This part of town was only slightly less known for its drug problems than the area where the Aggrettis lived.

But if Travis were involved in drugs, Clay would know and he would have used words a little stronger than ''bad'' to describe him. Whatever his objection to

Travis, she was reasonably sure that it wasn't because Travis was a criminal.

Carrying the tote bag, she made her way up the cement walk. Age and the tree roots had buckled the pavement, making it necessary to pay close attention to where she stepped. The need didn't disappear when she reached the porch steps. They had sags to match the one in the roof and Angie tested each one before trusting her weight to it.

Standing at last before the front door, she drew a deep breath and reminded herself that there was no reason she shouldn't be there. The mental pep talk did little to still the butterflies in her stomach but, ignoring them, she rapped her knuckles against the door and waited.

She'd almost decided that he wasn't home when she heard the sound of the dead bolt sliding back. The door opened and her carefully planned little speech about checking on him flew completely out of her mind.

"Are you all right?" It was a foolish question. He was most certainly *not* all right. Though he was standing in the shadows, they weren't thick enough to hide the bruises on his face.

"Angel?" It was obvious that she was about the last person he'd expected to find on his doorstep. Later, Angie suspected that it was that surprise that served to get her in the door.

"Why didn't you come into the clinic?" she demanded, stepping across the threshold without waiting for an invitation.

"For what?" Travis stepped back automatically, letting her in. He surreptitiously took the gun he'd been holding behind the door and slipped it out of sight beneath a wrinkled shirt draped over a table.

"For what?" The look she turned on him was a combination of exasperation and disbelief. "How about to have yourself patched back together?"

"I'm okay." He pulled his head back uneasily as she reached for his chin. "What are you doing?"

"I'm going to torture you," she snapped. "What do you think I'm going to do?"

"I don't know. That's why I asked. What are you doing here?"

"I was worried about you. Those two guys in the suits didn't look particularly friendly. I wanted to make sure you were all right."

"I'm fine."

"And I'm Julia Roberts," she said, making it clear what she thought of his claim to good health.

"I thought she was a brunette."

"And I thought you had a brain. Sit down."

Travis sat. It was just that he'd been sleeping when she arrived, he told himself. That was why it seemed to take more effort than it was worth to argue with her. He was still groggy.

"Open your mouth."

He did, intending to protest, only to have her shove a thermometer between his lips.

"I don't have a fever," he mumbled, frowning fiercely at her.

"I don't think I have much faith in your medical opinions," she said, reaching for his wrist. "Any two-year-old would have had the good sense to put some antiseptic on those cuts."

"I did," he protested around the thermometer.

"Well, you didn't do a very good job. The one above your left eyebrow is inflamed. Your pulse is up a bit."

"I'm not surprised." He discovered it was impossible to sound really scathing while talking around a thermometer. He would have taken it out but something in the set of her face suggested that she'd simply stick it back in.

He settled for frowning at her to make his annoyance known. She seemed singularly unimpressed. She withdrew the thermometer and frowned at it before shaking it down with an efficient flick of her wrist and sliding it back into its case.

"Your temperature is normal."

"I know," he said with awful sarcasm. She ignored him.

"You're lucky I came prepared," she said, bending to rummage through the tote she'd set on the floor.

"You shouldn't be here at all." He shifted restlessly on the old sofa, looking for a spot where the springs didn't seem quite so likely to pop through the fabric. "How did you find out where I lived, anyway?"

"Mrs. Aggretti. She told me you asked her to come by and clean for you once a week and that you paid her in advance. Several weeks in advance. That was the money you gave her when we were there."

"If I'd just given it to her, it would have looked like charity," he muttered, avoiding her eyes.

Angie's critical look took in the articles of clothing that had been allowed to fall where they would. Not that the decor would have been improved much by their absence. Early American Thrift Shop was the best description she could come up with. Nothing matched anything else. In fact, most of it didn't look as if it had *ever* matched anything else.

"Well, from the looks of this place, you can certainly use a cleaning lady."

"I haven't felt much like doing spring cleaning," Travis snapped defensively.

"If you'd come into the clinic and let me patch you up when this happened, maybe you *would* have felt like it." Angie glared at him, a tube of antiseptic clutched in her hand as if she were considering stabbing him with it.

Travis was the first to see the humor in the picture they made. The storm-cloud gray eased from his eyes, leaving the clear green behind as his mouth started to curve up.

"I don't think I've ever seen anyone make medicine look quite so threatening," he said, eyeing the antiseptic uneasily.

"I don't think I've ever had a patient who was so stubborn," Angie shot back but she eased her grip on the tube.

"Pax?" He held up his hand, giving her his most appealing smile.

"Pax."

Travis tried not to wince as her fingers closed over his bruised knuckles. But he apparently wasn't as stoic as he'd hoped because Angie's forehead creased, her eyes turning dark and worried again.

"What have you done to your hand?" She was already looking at it, taking in the scraped knuckles and swollen fingers. The look she threw him was a mixture of reproach and sympathy.

"They had very hard jaws," Travis offered by way of excuse.

"Grown men should not be finding out how hard the jaws of other grown men are by getting into fights with them," she scolded. But the bite had gone out of her voice. "Besides, there were two of them."

"So I noticed."

A shaft of sunlight had managed to find its way through a crack in the dusty curtains. It fell across her hair, painting a streak of pure gold across the honey blond.

"You're lucky you weren't hurt even worse." She dabbed antiseptic on the cut above his eyebrow.

"They didn't come out of it scot-free." There was pure, masculine satisfaction in the words. But it vanished instantly. "Ouch!"

"Sorry." She gave him a sweet, insincere smile. "I slipped."

"I thought maybe you were trying to finish what they started," he muttered, giving her a suspicious look.

"Don't be such a baby," she said briskly. "Turn your head so I can get to the cut on your chin."

Travis obeyed warily but her touch was gentle. He'd told her the truth when he said he was all right. He'd been banged up enough times to know the difference between painful but minor injuries and wounds in need of medical attention.

Still, maybe there was something to be said for medical attention, he thought, watching Angie's hair swing forward to frame her face as she leaned toward him. She was wearing the same soft perfume that she'd worn the first time they met. Wildflowers on a sunny day.

"Who were they?" Angie asked.

"Who were who?" The look she shot him said that she recognized deliberate obtuseness when she heard it.

"Those two 'business' associates of yours. The ones with the hard jaws," she clarified.

"No one important." He shrugged, trying not to wince when the movement reminded him of assorted bruises.

She was wearing a blouse of pale buttercup yellow, a plain style that tucked neatly into the waistband of an off-white skirt. The outfit was simple, clearly not designed for enticement. So why did he feel so thoroughly enticed?

"Don't you ever wear a uniform?" The question came out almost as an accusation and he saw the surprise in Angie's eyes as she answered.

"I worked the morning shift at the clinic today and I changed before I left. Is there something wrong with what I'm wearing?"

"I've just never seen you in a uniform." *And he'd never heard himself sound quite so much like a grumpy five-year-old.*

He allowed her to wrap gauze around his knuckles and tried not to wonder if the skin on her shoulders was as silky smooth as he'd imagined it to be. She was so close. He had only to reach out to be touching the buttons on her blouse.

"Take off your shirt."

"What?" His eyes jerked to hers. Was it possible that she'd read his mind?

"Take off your shirt," she repeated.

"Why?"

"Don't sound so suspicious. I'm not contemplating anything risqué."

"Too bad."

"I want to look at your ribs," she continued, ignoring his wistful comment.

"My ribs are fine." But he was reaching for the buttons on his shirt, knowing that she wasn't going to take his word for it.

"You'll forgive me if I don't accept your medical judgment."

Angie sat down on the sofa as he eased the shirt off his shoulders. Both were sitting at an angle, their knees touching. Not that it mattered, she reminded herself. Right now, Travis was only a patient. She reminded herself of that again as the shirt fell to the floor.

In her work, she'd seen her share of men's chests. She'd long since stopped seeing them as anything more than another part to be bandaged. She'd once told her friend Leigh that if Tom Selleck were to walk into the clinic she could tend to any injuries and never once notice him as a man.

Well, the jury was still out on Tom Selleck, but there was no question that her professional indifference did not hold up when it came to Travis Morgan. It had been hard enough to keep her mind on her work before he took his shirt off.

"You've got some nasty bruises," she said, aware that her voice was too breathy.

"Getting punched tends to do that to you."

The reminder of how he'd been hurt helped to steady her hands as she set them against his sides.

"Why did those men come after you?" Maybe if she focused on something unpleasant, she'd be able to forget how warm his skin felt.

"A business problem," Travis said. He sucked in a sharp breath as her fingers probed a particularly nasty bruise along his rib cage.

"What kind of business are you in that you settle problems with a fight? Most people take them to court."

"I do odds and ends. Nothing specific. I guess I'm like my father in that my attention span tends to be short so I don't stick with any one thing very long."

"Am I going to live?"

And that was all he was going to say about his "business," Angie thought. So be it. She wasn't going to pry. At least not now.

"I think you'll live. One of those ribs might be cracked." She ran her fingers along the rib in question. "It wouldn't hurt to have an X ray."

"It'll heal." He was so close, she could feel his breath stirring the tendrils of hair on her forehead.

"I could wrap it for you." Her fingers lingered on his side.

"No thanks. I'll be careful."

"Why do I doubt that?" she asked, lifting her eyes to his.

"Because you're the suspicious sort?" His hand came up to brush the hair back from her face. "When the sunlight hits your hair, it turns it the most incredible shade of gold."

"It's just blond."

"It's beautiful."

"Thank you." When had he gotten closer? He was so close that she could see the tiny gray lines that radiated out from his pupils, adding depth to the clear green of his eyes. And why were her hands still lingering on his skin?

"You know, we were interrupted the other day," he said.

"We were?" His fingers were drifting down the side of her neck. Angie swallowed hard and tried to ignore the delicious shiver that worked its way along her spine.

"Where were we?" Travis murmured, drawing closer still.

"I don't know," she lied. She could feel her pulse beating in her throat, harder and faster than it had any right to be.

"I think we were just about . . . here." The last word was spoken against her mouth.

Angie's eyes fell shut, her lashes suddenly much too heavy. Travis's mouth feathered over hers in a kiss as soft as a butterfly's wing. She sighed, her lips parting in an unconscious invitation. An invitation he accepted.

His hand cupped the back of her neck as his head angled to deepen the kiss. Angie felt as if her bones were melting. Her tongue came up to meet his, touching shyly and then withdrawing only to be drawn irresistibly forward again.

Her hands slipped lightly up his chest to his shoulders, her fingers curling into the corded muscles there. Her head tilted back in complete surrender as she opened herself to him.

Her rational mind could argue all it wanted that she barely knew this man, that two meetings hardly constituted enough of an acquaintance for them to be necking on the sofa like teenagers. But rational arguments couldn't compete with the way he made her feel.

Tasting her total surrender, Travis moved to pull her still closer, so close that not even a shadow could slip between them. But the movement ended abruptly when his bruised ribs protested with a sharp stab of pain.

"Damn." The word came out on a groan as he jerked back. The abrupt movement startled another groan from him.

"Are you all right? Where does it hurt?" In an instant, the passionate woman disappeared and was replaced by the nurse. The transformation made Travis want to groan again.

"I'm fine. It's my ribs that have a problem," he said ruefully.

"You should have X rays," she fretted.

"There's nothing broken. And if there were, I suspect a few more kisses like that would patch me up." He reached to pull her back into his arms, but Angie stood up and out of reach.

"I really should get going," she mumbled, pushing things back into her tote.

Travis opened his mouth to try to persuade her to stay but closed it without saying anything. She shouldn't have come here in the first place. He should have made her leave immediately. Instead, he'd let her fuss over injuries too minor to mention and he'd compounded his error by kissing her in a way that left no doubt about just how much he wanted her. Maybe he'd taken one too many blows to the head.

He stood up and followed her to the door. Angie stopped in the doorway, turning back to look at him, her expression worried.

"You'll take it easy, won't you? You need to rest those ribs."

"Yes, Nurse. I'll be good." Though he told himself not to, his hand came up, his fingers brushing over her cheek. "Thanks for the concern. It's been a long time since anyone fussed over me." *As in, never,* he thought.

"Well, everyone ought to be fussed over occasionally," she said briskly. She hesitated a moment and then rose on her toes to press a quick kiss to his mouth, drawing away before he could respond.

"Just to help the healing process," she said, her tone light, even though her cheeks were flushed.

Travis watched her walk to the curb, waiting until she was safely in her car and pulling away. He shut the door and leaned back against it, his expression thoughtful. He was probably making a big mistake. Reason said that Angie Brady was a complication he couldn't afford.

For her sake, as well as for the business he had to do in Salem, he would take care that their paths didn't cross again.

But for the first time in a very long time, he was in no mood to listen to the voice of reason. He was listening instead to gut-level instincts that told him not to walk away from this—that he'd regret it for the rest of his life if he did.

Chapter Five

Travis paced the stark room with long, restless strides. He didn't like police stations—he never had. He especially didn't like viewing them from the wrong side of a holding cell. He knew exactly what was going on but that didn't make him like it any more.

There was no clock on the wall and he wasn't wearing a watch, so he didn't know the time but he knew he'd been pacing this damn room long enough to put considerable wear on his shoes. Hell of a way to get his exercise, he thought, his mouth curving with wry humor.

Hearing the door open behind him, he spun on one heel, his expression tightening when he saw who entered.

"Brady." His tone was flat, his eyes cold and hard.

"Morgan." Clay's tone was no warmer than Travis's. He didn't say anything more, allowing the silence in the small room to thicken.

"I guess you didn't have me called in to chat about the good old days," Travis said finally. He pushed his hands into the pockets of his jeans and leaned his shoulders on the gray wall behind him, looking as comfortable as if he were chatting with a friend.

"Where were you yesterday?" Clay asked abruptly.

"I was around. Why are you asking?"

"Someone stole a Ferrari yesterday afternoon."

"Too bad. What does it have to do with me?" There was no sign of tension allowed to show in Travis's cool gaze.

"The theft has your fingerprints all over it."

"But does the car?" Travis lifted one brow in cool question.

"We haven't found the car yet," Clay admitted grudgingly. "But the M.O. looks like your style."

"I didn't realize you'd studied my 'style.' I'm flattered."

"Don't be," Clay snapped. "Where were you yesterday afternoon around three o'clock?"

I was kissing your sister, Travis thought. But he decided it wouldn't be politic to say as much.

"I was at home," he said.

"I suppose you just happened to be alone so there wouldn't be any witnesses who could corroborate," Clay suggested sarcastically.

"You know, jumping to conclusions can be a dangerous business."

"Are you saying you weren't alone?" Clay didn't bother to disguise the disappointment he felt at learning that Travis might have an alibi.

Travis shrugged. Damn jealous brothers all to hell. Having Brady drag him in here this way could ruin everything he'd been working toward. And if he told him that Brady's own sister was his alibi, it was only going to make the man more determined to bring him down, if not with this, then with something else.

"If you've got an alibi, you're going to need it," Clay said.

"Not unless you've got something more concrete than the fact that you don't like me." Travis straightened away from the wall, pulling his hands from his pockets, letting his temper show for the first time. "You can't keep me away from your sister by trumping up charges against me, Brady."

"I'll do whatever I have to, Morgan." Clay set his palms on the table and leaned toward Travis, his eyes an angry blue. "I don't want you near Angie."

"Too bad you don't have much to say about it," Travis said, his tone a taunt.

"You haven't changed, Morgan. I don't know how you've managed to convince Angie to give you the time of day but I'm not going to stand back and watch you use her. If I can't nail you on this theft, I'll find something else."

"Careful, *Officer* Brady." Travis's eyes were as cold as Clay's were hot. "False arrest charges won't look good on your record. You've got nothing on me and you and I both know it."

"You were part of a car-theft ring twelve years ago," Clay snapped.

"Prove it."

"You met with Shearson."

"So what? Is it illegal to have a drink with an old acquaintance?" *Damn Shearson and his need to flaunt his activities in front of the noses of the police.*

"The only acquaintances Shearson has are the flunkies who deal drugs for him."

"You're entitled to your opinion." Travis shrugged tightly.

"Stay away from my sister," Clay told him, abandoning any pretense that he wasn't personally involved.

"She's old enough to take care of herself."

"Not with you, she isn't." Clay straightened away from the table, his hands clenching into fists. "She doesn't have any more business getting involved with you than a baby has playing in the street."

Under the anger and dislike was worry. Travis had never had a sister to worry about—or anyone else, for that matter—but it wasn't difficult to empathize with what Clay was feeling. There wasn't anything Clay could say about the unsuitability of Travis's relationship with his sister that Travis hadn't already said to himself.

Feeling suddenly intensely weary, Travis thrust his fingers through his hair, wanting nothing more than to go home and take a hot shower. This arrest had probably already blown everything all to hell and there was nothing he could do about that. All he wanted was to get out of there—immediately, if not sooner.

He could just tell Brady that he'd stay away from Angie—it was what he should have done anyway. And then maybe he could go home and start figuring out how much damage had been done by his arrest. He had to call Shearson, who'd undoubtedly known about the arrest as soon as it happened.

Before he could say anything, the door opened and a thin-faced man appeared in the doorway. Clay turned, impatient at the interruption. The newcomer gestured him over.

Without seeming to pay too much attention, Travis watched the two men. Obviously *he* was the main topic of conversation. Equally obvious was the fact that Brady didn't like whatever he was hearing. Travis could see the line of his jaw harden like iron as he listened to what the other man was saying. He shot back a few rapid sentences and then turned back to Travis as the other man withdrew.

"You're free to go, Morgan." The words were so tight and hard, they practically qualified as weapons.

"Find the real thief?" Travis asked, arching one brow.

"No. The word came down to let you go. It seems you have friends."

"Everybody ought to have one or two." Even as he spoke, his mind was working furiously.

Why hadn't they just left him to deal with this on his own? Brady hadn't had enough to hold him. A few more minutes of hassle and it would have been settled. Now, Brady had proof, if he'd needed it, that Travis was a less-than-model citizen. Not that he gave a damn what Clay Brady thought of him.

But he gave more than a damn about what his sister thought, Travis admitted bleakly.

"Well, it's been swell, but I'm sure you'll understand if I cut this short." Nothing of his thoughts showed in his expression as he moved toward the door Clay had opened. They stepped into the hall together.

"This isn't over, Morgan," Clay promised tightly.

"There's somebody here to see you, Brady." A tall Hispanic officer interrupted them before Travis could respond.

"Tell them I'll be there in a minute, Martinez," Clay said without taking his eyes from Travis.

"It's your sister." His words riveted their attention to his face. He cleared his throat uneasily. "She says this guy's got an alibi for yesterday afternoon."

"What?" The word was more an expression of disbelief than a question but Martinez answered Clay anyway.

"She says she was with him."

The words fell like a rock into a still pool, sending out waves at their impact.

Dammit, Angel, why didn't you keep your mouth shut. He'd managed to avoid mentioning her presence to her brother. There was no reason for anyone to know she'd been with him. Now, the whole world would know. Why hadn't he listened to his own excellent advice and kept his distance from her at the start? What was it about those big blue eyes and soft mouth that short-circuited his brain?

But all that showed in his expression was a sort of smirking triumph.

"I told you I had an alibi, Brady."

The look Clay turned on him should have incinerated him on the spot. When Clay turned away without a word, Travis knew it was because he didn't trust himself to speak. He followed Clay. Angie was waiting at the end of the hallway, her expression a mixture of nerves and determination.

"Hello, Angel." Travis spoke first, his tone intimate. "What's a nice girl like you doing in a place like this?"

"Making sure justice is served," Angie said, her eyes darting over him, as if to make sure he was all right.

"You can stop looking for bruises, Angie," Clay said, his voice a little too tight for humor. "I haven't used a rubber hose on a prisoner in months."

"Travis was with me yesterday afternoon," she said, not bothering to respond to Clay's comment.

"So Martinez said." Clay shot a sharp look at Travis, silently promising retribution.

"We were at his house," Angie added for good measure.

"At his house?" Clay's expression grew positively threatening.

"How did you know where I was, Angel?" Travis reached out to brush a lock of hair back from Angie's face in a move calculated to make her brother's blood pressure rise. Damn Clay Brady, anyway. Who was he to judge the rest of the world?

"Mrs. Aggretti told me. She brought the baby into the clinic this afternoon and said you'd been arrested." Angie's eyes told him that she knew exactly who his intimate little gesture had been intended to impress.

"I appreciate your coming to my rescue."

"I just wanted to make sure the police had all the facts."

"Very civic-minded of you, sis." Clay's smile was tight. "Could I speak to you for a minute?"

Angie hesitated. She didn't want to hear another lecture on Travis's unsuitability. On the other hand, maybe if she let Clay get it off his chest now, she wouldn't have to listen to it at home later. With an apologetic smile to Travis, she allowed her brother to draw her aside.

"What are you doing here?" he demanded as they stopped next to an unoccupied desk.

"I told you. I was with Travis yesterday, during the time Mrs. Aggretti said the car was stolen."

"So you rushed down here to rescue him from the evil clutches of the police?"

"No. I rushed down here to make sure you didn't throw him in jail on some trumped-up charge just to keep him away from me," she snapped.

"It wasn't a trumped-up charge." He ground out the words.

"Good." She refused to look apologetic about suggesting that he'd abuse his badge. "Is he free to go now that you know he didn't commit a crime?"

"All I *know* is that he didn't steal a car," Clay corrected her.

"Are you going to let him go?" she asked with steely emphasis.

"Unfortunately I don't have a choice. Wait." He caught her arm when she started to turn away.

"What?" Angie waited. She couldn't remember ever feeling such an enormous gap between them. Clay must have felt something of the same thing because his expression softened.

"I don't want to fight with you about this, sis."

"Good. Because I don't want to fight you."

"Can't you just take my word for it when I tell you to keep your distance from Travis Morgan?" His tone held more plea than demand.

"Not unless you can give me something a little more concrete than he's a 'bad man.'" She set her hand over his and looked up at him, trying to make him understand. "I'm a big girl, Clay. I don't need my big brother to shield me from every bump and scrape anymore. I can take care of myself. Trust me."

"It's not you I don't trust. And you're heading for a lot more than a skinned knee," Clay said, looking over her shoulder to where Travis lounged insolently against the edge of a counter.

"He's not as wicked as he looks," Angie told him, following his eyes.

"What makes you so sure?" He searched her face, finding nothing there to reassure him. She looked, he thought despairingly, much too much like a woman about to fall in love. If she wasn't already there.

"I just don't want to see you hurt," he said, knowing the words sounded lame but helpless to come up with anything stronger.

"You can't protect me forever, Clay. You've got to let me make my own mistakes. *If* this is a mistake," she added.

It was a mistake, all right, he thought as he watched his sister leave with Travis. Just as a moth hovering too close to an open flame, Angie was likely to get her wings badly singed.

TRAVIS STARED out the windshield, oblivious to his cramped legs. He was only half aware that Angie had remembered to start a conversation twice, only to give up in the face of his monosyllabic responses. He couldn't stop thinking about her expression when she'd seen him in the police station—the worry in her eyes, her anger over what seemed to her an unjust arrest.

And he couldn't forget Brady's expression as he'd looked at the two of them together. Brady was convinced that he was going to cause his sister nothing but heartache. And the hell of it was he couldn't argue otherwise.

Travis shifted restlessly in the narrow seat, his forehead pleating in a frown. It was ironic that Angie's arrival had provided him with the alibi Brady had been so sure he didn't have.

She was handy, no arguing that. If he continued to see her, he'd find his business somewhat easier. Even the fact that she was a cop's sister could be worked to his advantage.

"You're awfully quiet." The glance she slid him was questioning.

"Not much to say." Travis lifted one shoulder in a half shrug, keeping his eyes on the unimpressive view out the window.

Angie stopped the car next to the curb in front of his rented house and shut off the engine. Travis looked at the old house, suddenly noticing just how shabby it was. It had probably been a nice home when it was new but time and neglect had taken a harsh toll. It needed a good coat of paint and a new roof, he thought. Maybe a fence to take the place of the dying box-woods that lined the cracked sidewalk.

Listen to him. He was starting to sound like Mr. Average American, worried about sprucing up the home. Only it wasn't his home, any more than any other place had ever been his home. He was just passing through this house, just as he'd passed through other houses and apartments in his time. Once this job was done, he'd be moving out and the place would be forgotten inside of a month.

"Are you okay?" Angie's worried tone made Travis realize that he'd been sitting there, staring out the window, like a man in a trance.

"Sure. I'm fine." He turned to look at her, one side of his mouth curling up in a half smile. "I really appreciate you coming to the station and the lift back here." His tone was cool, impersonal.

"I was upset when Mrs. Aggretti told me what had happened. Why didn't you tell Clay you were with me?"

"It's bad policy to tell a cop that you were with his sister when the crime in question was committed," he said, shrugging indifferently. "It tends to make them testy."

"But they would have let you go sooner."

"I didn't have anything important to do this morning anyway," he said. "Thanks again." He reached for the door handle.

"Aren't you going to invite me in?" Angie's tone was light but he heard the uncertainty behind the question.

"It's not a good time," he said coolly. "I've got things to do." He turned to look at her, steeling himself against the temptation of those big blue eyes. "Actually I'm going to be pretty busy for quite a while."

He saw the impact of the blatant brush-off in the way her eyes darkened, heard it in the soft catch of her breath. It was for the best, he reminded himself, meeting her searching look with cool indifference.

"If this is because of Clay . . . because of something he said to you, I'd like to point out that I'm old enough to run my own life."

"I've dealt with big brothers before, Angel. And I haven't let one scare me off yet."

"Then why are you trying to get rid of me?"

The humor in her voice couldn't hide the hurt she felt and Travis had to fight the urge to kiss that look from her eyes. Damn. When had he gotten in so deep? He hadn't known her that long. He had no business caring about her feelings as much as he did.

"Don't make a big deal out of it," he said, his tone careless enough to be an insult. "I've just got some things to do for the next few days. I'll call you."

He pushed open the door and got out of the car before those eyes of hers could make him change his mind. It was for her own good, he reminded himself as he strode up the buckled walkway. She wasn't the sort of woman who could have a casual affair and then walk away unscathed. Besides, he didn't need any distractions right now. Better to get her out of the way so he could get on with his job.

He was slipping his key into the front door before he heard Angie's car start. A moment later, she pulled away from the curb and Travis couldn't keep from turning to watch the little compact zip down the street. He watched it until it was out of sight, trying to ignore the sinking feeling that he'd just made the biggest mistake of his life.

Chapter Six

"Eight ball. Side pocket." Travis waited for his opponent's acknowledgement before he leaned down to make the shot. He eased the cue stick back and then sent it forward with a quick jab. The ball ghosted by the eight ball, barely kissing it. With an almost lazy air, the black ball rolled into the side pocket as if there'd never been any question about where it was going.

"Man, you've got the best damn luck I ever seen." The complaint was good-natured as the other man handed over the twenty dollars that had been riding on the game.

"Skill, my man. Luck doesn't make shots like that. It's pure skill."

"Well, whatever it is, I can't afford to lose any more money to you tonight. My old lady's gonna kill me as it is."

Travis grinned and waved the waitress over to order two more beers. "My treat," he told the other man.

"The least I can do is buy you a drink before the funeral."

"It might help to numb the pain a little." His erstwhile opponent laughed and took the beer the waitress offered before he wandered off to watch a poker game in progress in one of the booths.

Travis chalked the end of his cue stick, his eyes skimming restlessly over the crowd that filled the Bucket of Blood. Most of them were locals. The Bucket of Blood was not the kind of establishment that made it onto lists of places to visit while in Salem.

It was a neighborhood hangout without any of the coziness that would have gone along with that title in a better neighborhood. Fistfights were the rule but they rarely amounted to much. The bartender, who was also the owner, kept a baseball bat and a shotgun behind the bar and he didn't like it when his furniture was damaged. Even the most acrimonious battle came to a screeching halt when Sal came out from behind his bar with the bat in one hand and the shotgun in the other. As far as Travis knew, he'd never used the shotgun but the same couldn't be said for the bat.

Sal's presence tended to encourage a certain amount of order if not decorum. Fights were politely moved outside if they threatened to become too vigorous.

"You could chalk your stick at my place, sugar." The woman who spoke was wearing a pair of shiny silver spandex pants and a black knit top that was hardly more than a bandage. Her heavily made-up eyes gave out an unmistakable invitation.

"No, thanks."

"I've got some real nice chalk, sugar." She walked her fingers up his arm, looking up at him from beneath a pair of false eyelashes the size of awnings. "Won't cost you as much as losing one of those silly old bets would."

"But I'm not losing." Travis grinned at her and shifted away so that her hand fell from his arm. He reached into his pocket and pulled out a five-dollar bill. "Here. Have a couple of drinks on me."

The woman looked surprised but she took the money from him with a quick gesture that said she was afraid he might change his mind if she hesitated. Travis turned back to the table as she moved away. Even if he'd been inclined to accept her invitation, an image of wide-set blue eyes and hair the color of sunshine would have intruded.

He began racking the balls, setting up a new game, wanting nothing more than to go home. Funny, how when he thought of going home, he suddenly pictured his grandfather's huge house. He'd had such high hopes when he arrived there. Despite the shock of losing his parents, there'd been a secret, guilty excitement when he thought of finally having a home—a real home. It hadn't taken him long to figure out that there was more to a home than simply staying in one place for more than a few months.

He shook off the unpleasant memories and slid the racked balls into place before lifting the rack slowly from them. It was all a long time ago and far, far away, to quote George Lucas. He had better things to think about, such as how to get one blond, blue-eyed nurse out of his thoughts.

"Quarter a ball. Your choice of games."

Travis stiffened, his fingers curling over the rack. Now he was hearing things. It had to be his imagination because there was no way on earth that Angie Brady was standing behind him, challenging him to a game of pool. No way that she was in the Bucket of Blood. No way that she'd have sought him out after the way he'd dismissed her last week. He turned slowly.

And Angie stood there smiling at him.

She was wearing jeans and a hot pink T-shirt. Her hair was caught back from her face and held at the base of her neck by a blue-and-pink polka-dot bow. She looked fresh and young and as out of place as a kitten in a mud puddle.

And he'd never seen anything more desirable in his life.

"What are you doing here?"

"I felt like a game of pool." Angie grinned at him, feeling her confidence take a much needed jump upward. She'd stopped here on an impulse when she'd seen Travis's bike out front.

She couldn't believe she was here. She'd never been in a bar like this in her life. It seemed as if, since she'd met Travis, she was doing all kinds of things she'd never considered doing before.

She'd questioned her own sanity in seeking him after the way he'd pushed her away. But for an instant she saw something in his eyes that told her she'd done the right thing.

"You play here often?" he asked, indicating their rough surroundings.

"All the time," she lied breezily. "I'm something of a pool trout, you know."

"A pool trout?" Travis's brows climbed upward, a hint of laughter in his eyes. "No kidding."

"I can see you don't believe me," she said, feigning indignation. "You think I'm lying."

"I didn't say that." But there was a suspicious tuck in his cheek that gave the lie to his serious expression.

"Are you going to play or do I have to find someone who isn't afraid of me?" Angie tilted her chin, giving him a challenging look.

Of course he wasn't going to actually play a game of pool with her, Travis told himself. He was going to usher her politely but firmly out of the Bucket of Blood. He'd make sure she got into her car and went back where she belonged. Where she was safe.

"Eight ball. Fifty bucks a game." He saw Angie's eyes widen, whether at his agreement or at the stakes he couldn't tell. But she swallowed once and nodded.

"Fine. Can you give me one of those stick thingies?"

Stick thingies? Oh, they were certainly in for a challenging game. He got a cue stick off the wall rack and chalked the end before handing it to her.

"Thanks." Angie set the beer she'd ordered on a table nearby and took the stick from him.

"Do you want to break?" Travis asked politely.

"No, thank you. I always have a hard time getting the balls apart." She smiled up at him and Travis felt something dangerously warm unfold in his chest. He turned away before he could give in to the urge to do something remarkably stupid. Something such as kissing her right in front of God and the patrons of the Bucket of Blood.

He aligned the cue ball and broke, scattering the balls across the table. The fifteen spun into a pocket but he missed the next shot. Probably because his mind was more on the woman behind him than on the game, he admitted ruefully.

"You've got solids," he said.

"The ones with almost no white on them?" she asked, eyeing the table uncertainly.

"The ones with almost no white on them," he confirmed, biting his lip against the urge to grin. Maybe she'd described herself better than she knew when she said she was a pool trout. He suspected a fish might know just about as much about the game.

Angie circled the table warily, eyeing the balls as if they were made of plastique. When she finally settled on a shot, she edged up to the table and set her hand on the green felt, balancing the cue stick on top of her fingers in a way that was guaranteed to end in a missed shot at least, torn felt at the worst.

"You know, there are easier ways to hold a pool stick," Travis said, coming up behind her.

"There are?" She straightened and looked at him. "I've always done okay with *my* way."

"That doesn't mean it's the best way." *If she'd ever hit a ball with a hold like that, he'd eat the table.* "I could show you if you'd like."

She hesitated, as if considering and then nodded. "Okay."

It wasn't until Travis had put his hands on hers that it occurred to him that showing her how to shoot pool meant practically embracing her. With his right arm laid along hers, her back snuggled invitingly against his chest as they leaned over the table.

"Put your hand like this," he told her, trying not to notice how soft her skin was. "And hold the stick in your other hand like this."

She smelled like a spring meadow, all sunshine and flowers. It took a real effort to resist the urge to turn his face into her hair.

"Like this?" She turned her head to look at him, so close that it would take only a small movement to bring their mouths together. Travis saw his own awareness reflected in her eyes. His hands tightened over hers, his arms drew her imperceptibly closer. Another heartbeat and he'd be able to taste the sweet warmth of her lips.

"Like that." He released her as if he'd been about to embrace a cactus, stepping back for good measure. "Do you think you have it now?"

"I think so," Angie said. She cleared her throat and turned her attention back to the table. "I think I understand, now."

"Good." Travis decided it was safer not to ask just what it was she understood. He hoped it was only the hold he'd shown her.

The first shot was so easy he felt no surprise when she made it. Angie seemed as pleased as a child when the ball hit the pocket and Travis raised his beer in salute. The second shot was a little tougher but not beyond the realm of beginner's luck. The third shot was something else altogether. It was his first real clue that things might not be what they seemed.

He set his beer down and leaned forward, watching in disbelief as she banked the cue ball and sent it spinning into the four with a smooth ease that wouldn't have shamed a professional. Her smile seemed a little less childlike this time. She paused to take a swallow of beer and look at the table.

"I have a feeling I've been suckered," Travis commented, to no one in particular.

"I don't know what you mean." She blinked at him, her eyes pure innocence.

She returned to the table without waiting for an answer. Travis watched with resigned amusement as she ran the table, knocking balls into pockets with an ease that spoke of considerable practice.

"Eight ball, corner pocket," she announced confidently. He was not in the least surprised to see the eight ball disappear into the stated pocket.

"I suppose this will teach me not to be overconfident." He reached into his pocket as she approached, pulling out the required number of bills.

"I guess I did pretty good, huh?" Angie's smile was all innocence as she took the money from him and tucked it into the pocket of her jeans.

"Not bad for a pool trout," he commented dryly. "I think you got the wrong fish, by the way. Shark might be a little more accurate."

"Shark. Trout. I always get those two confused." She fluttered her lashes at him.

"One has much bigger teeth. And I think I know which one bit me." He signaled the waitress for another beer for Angie, who'd just finished hers.

"I did tell you I was good," she pointed out virtuously.

"Yeah. And you were careful to do it in a way that made sure I wouldn't believe you. Where'd you learn to play like that? And don't tell me it was the Bucket of Blood because I don't think you've set foot in here before tonight."

"Why not? Do I look out of place?"

"No more than a glass of ice water in hell." Travis grinned at her disappointed expression. Didn't she realize how her freshness stood out in the smoke-filled room? She was like a ray of sunshine in a dungeon.

"Where did you learn to play?" he asked again.

"Clay taught me. But he won't play with me anymore," she added, with a suggestion of a pout.

"I can see why," Travis said dryly.

"I could give you a chance to recoup your loss," she suggested.

"You're trying to hustle me."

"I'm just trying to be fair. Of course, if you don't think you could beat me . . ." She let the challenge trail off.

He should send her home, he thought. She didn't belong here any more than she belonged with him.

Hadn't he been through all this last week? Playing pool with her was *not* the way to put distance between them.

"I'm not going to show you how to hold your stick this time," he warned her.

"I don't need anyone to show me how to hold a stick, Travis." The look she shot him from under her lashes gave double meaning to the words.

It was the second time in thirty minutes that he'd been more or less propositioned. But whereas the first woman had left him with nothing but a vague feeling of pity, the playful invitation in Angie's eyes had an altogether different effect.

How was he supposed to do the right thing and keep her at a distance when she gave him a look like that?

ANGIE CERTAINLY didn't need any instruction in the fine art of shooting pool. Travis understood completely why her brother no longer played with her. There was something disconcerting about competing with someone who looked like Cinderella and played like Minnesota Fats.

She insisted on referring to the solids as "the balls with hardly any white on them" and she held her stick the way a three-year-old would. But it didn't seem to matter. It was as if she charmed the balls into going where she wanted them. Not that Travis blamed them. She could have charmed him into doing just about anything she wanted.

How else could he explain the fact that he hadn't marched her out of the Bucket of Blood and sent her safely home? He'd spent the past week thinking about her far more than he had any business doing. He'd almost managed to convince himself that she was forgotten. And then she turned up where he least expected her and made him realize just how much he'd been lying to himself.

"LAST CALL." The waitress leaned one hip against the pool table, easing the weight on her feet.

"Last call?" Travis looked at her in surprise before glancing at his watch. One-thirty in the morning. He'd lost all track of time—not a healthy habit for someone in his profession. He and Angie had been playing pool since nine.

"You want another beer?" The waitress sounded impatient. Though the crowd had thinned out, there were still enough customers to make the last half hour of her shift a busy one.

"No, thanks." Travis dropped a five on her tray, a generous tip for the night's service. He nodded absently in answer to her thanks. His attention was on Angie, who was weaving her way back from the rest room.

And "weaving" was the operative word, he realized. She wasn't simply working her way between the crowded tables, she also seemed to be having some difficulty putting one foot in front of the other. How much had she had to drink tonight? He narrowed his eyes as he tried to remember. Four...maybe five beers. More than enough for someone who wasn't accustomed to drinking.

"Ready for another game?" she asked as she reached the table.

"I think it's time to call it quits," Travis said.

"I'm still two games ahead of you. Don't you want to try to even the score? Where's my drink?" She looked down, frowning when she didn't find it.

"You finished it. And I'm willing to postpone the rematch. I think it's time you went home."

"Why?" She peered up at him, her eyes ever so slightly glazed. "Afraid I'll beat you again?"

"It's possible." Though at the moment, it seemed unlikely that she could hit the broadside of a barn with a truck. When had she gotten so high? And why hadn't he realized what was happening sooner? *Because he hadn't wanted to. Because he'd been enjoying himself and he hadn't wanted the evening to end.*

"Come on. You need to get home." He found her purse and handed it to her.

"But I was having fun," she protested, looking over her shoulder at the pool table as he was ushering her out the door.

"Yes, but it's late and if I don't get you home, your brother will probably track me down and blow my head off."

"Oh, Clay." She puckered her face in a disparaging look that made Travis want to kiss her. "He's a worrywart."

"Yeah, well, if I had a sister, I'd be a worrywart, too."

"Nope. You're not the type." She spun away from him suddenly and threw her arms up as if to embrace the full moon that hung overhead. "I feel like dancing."

"Too bad. You're going home." Travis caught hold of her arm and tugged her over to where his bike was parked.

"What about my car?" She dragged back, frowning at him.

"You're the one who told me no one would bother it around here. I can't say the same about my bike. And you're in no condition to drive."

She continued to frown but allowed him to lead her to the motorcycle. Travis had carried his helmet from the bar and now he lifted it and set it over her head.

"You're really making a habit of this, you know."

"I know. Do you mind?" She looked up at him, all eyes and soft mouth and Travis had to fight the urge to kiss her.

"I don't mind," he said gruffly. God help him, he didn't mind at all.

He drove her home through streets made quiet by the late hour. Angie snuggled against his back, her arms looped intimately around his waist. It would have been easy to pretend that they were just an ordinary couple, going home after an evening with friends. They'd go up to bed and Angie would cuddle against him as she fell asleep.

It was a lovely fantasy but Travis had never been inclined to play games of pretend. He'd spent a lot of lonely hours playing pretend when he was a child and he'd soon learned that reality always came crashing back in. It hurt less if you didn't pretend in the first place.

He eased to a halt in front of Angie's house and helped her off the bike. The ride hadn't sobered her. She stumbled on a nonexistent crack in the sidewalk and then giggled like a teenager at a slumber party.

"I think I had too much to drink," she informed him.

"So I noticed."

"I'm a little high." She seemed to think it was important to clarify her state.

"Just a little," he agreed, catching her arm when she stumbled again.

She giggled covering her mouth with one hand as she peered up at him in the moonlight. "I don't usually drink very much."

"No kidding." He sighed when she stumbled a third time. Setting one arm around her waist, he scooped her off her feet, cradling her against his chest.

"I can walk," she said. But she looped her arms around his neck and set her head on his shoulder.

"You seem to be doing a better job of falling at the moment."

He carried her up the walk, grateful that the moon was bright enough to light the way. There was a delay when he reached the door while Angie searched her purse for the keys. She found them at last, and dangled them triumphantly. Rather than wait while she attempted to insert the key in the lock, Travis set her down and did the job himself. Angie leaned against him, humming softly.

Once the door was open, he picked her up again and carried her into the entryway. There were no lights on and he could only hope that Brady was either not home or was a sound sleeper. If he found Travis carrying his half-conscious sister up the stairs, he was not going to be a happy camper.

Having negotiated the staircase, he pushed open the door Angie indicated and carried her into her bedroom. The moonlight that had been such a help outside couldn't penetrate through the curtains drawn over the windows. Rather than risk stumbling over something in the dark room, Travis lowered Angie to her feet and pushed the door shut behind them before groping for the light switch.

The switch lit a lamp that sat on an oak dresser. It illuminated a room that was pleasantly feminine without being full of ruffles and floral prints. The crisp blue-and-white stripes and light oak furniture were exactly right for Angie. The same soft practicality that he'd come to associate with her.

Angie began to slide down the door, reminding him that he wasn't here to critique the decor but to get Angie to bed. Lifting her again, he carried her to the bed and set her on her feet. Steadying her with an arm around her waist, he turned down the covers before easing her onto the bed.

She immediately flopped onto her back, throwing her arms out against the cool linens.

"I feel so good."

"Enjoy it while you can. You're probably going to feel like hell in the morning."

"Don't be a grouch." She grinned up at him and patted the bed invitingly. "Want to join me?"

Travis reached for one of her feet and began unlacing her sneaker with quick jerks. Somewhere, someone was having one hell of a good joke at his expense. *Did he want to join her?* Only about as much as he wanted to continue breathing.

When the second sneaker hit the floor, he straightened and considered her. Jeans were not the most comfortable garment to sleep in but there was a limit to his self-control. If he started removing more than her shoes, he was going to forget just how ungentlemanly it would be to take advantage of a woman who'd had too much to drink.

"Come on. Get under the covers."

Angie shifted obediently, laying her head on the pillow and allowing him to pull the covers up to her shoulders. But when he started to move away, she reached out and caught hold of his hand.

"Aren't you going to kiss me good-night?"

How was it possible for a woman to ask a question such as that and still manage to look as innocent as a child? On the other hand, how was it possible to resist the look in her eyes? It would take a stronger man than he was, Travis admitted without regret.

Her mouth was soft and warm, as sleepy as her eyes and even more tempting. It would be so easy to deepen the kiss, to take the next step and then the next . . . .

"Go to sleep," he said as he pulled back.

She looked up at him, her eyes smoky blue and mysterious in the soft light.

"Stay with me until I fall asleep."

Travis groaned. Just what had he done to deserve this kind of torture?

"That's not a good idea, Angel." He started to move away but she tightened her hold on his hand, pulling him closer.

"Please, Travis. Just stay until I fall asleep."

"No. I can't." There were limits to his willpower and he'd just about exceeded them with that kiss.

"Don't leave me alone."

The words touched off a flood of old memories. How many times had he asked his parents not to leave him alone in some new place? He heard the echo of those childish pleas in Angie's words and it was always followed by his mother's admonition not to be such a baby and then the closing of a door.

But this wasn't the same thing at all. He wasn't leaving Angie alone in some half-restored monastery in Thailand or a tent in South America. This was her own bedroom in the house she'd grown up in, with her brother probably asleep just down the hall. It wasn't the same thing at all.

"Please, Travis. Stay with me," she whispered again, her voice as soft as a siren's and just as irresistible.

"Just until you fall asleep," he said slowly, wondering where his sanity had gone. He looked around for a chair but she was pulling him toward the bed.

"You can lay on top of the covers," she said. She scooted into the middle of the bed to make room, looking up at him with such a bright expression that he had to believe she was either too naive or too drunk to know what she was doing.

Travis hesitated and then shrugged. "In for a penny, in for a pound," he muttered. If he was going to be tortured, he might as well be comfortable.

He stretched out gingerly, propping his shoulders against the oak headboard and setting his booted feet uneasily on top of the striped cotton spread.

"See? Isn't this better?" Angie promptly shifted over to snuggle against his side.

Better? Better than what, he wondered. It was marginally better than having bamboo shoots thrust under his fingernails. Or jumping from a plane at thirty-thousand feet without a parachute. The jury was still out on whether or not he'd prefer to walk on hot coals.

"This is nice," she murmured sleepily.

Well, "nice" was a relative term. If one considered slow torture nice, then he supposed this would qualify. He shifted lower so that she could rest her head on his shoulder. Her hair smelled of cigarette smoke from the bar but underneath that was the scent of sunshine.

Travis let his eyes drift shut. Just for a moment. As soon as he was sure she was asleep, he'd leave. He was really going to have to make her understand that she couldn't keep coming around. She was all sunshine and he was all shadow and the two simply weren't compatible.

He turned his face into her hair, his long body relaxing further into the mattress. Her brother was right when he told her that he was a bad man. And angels shouldn't mix with bad men.

Chapter Seven

Travis came awake slowly, aware that he hadn't slept long enough. Frowning, he turned his head into the pillow, courting a few more hours of sleep. The pillow shifted and murmured something low and indistinguishable. The urge for more sleep vanished instantly.

Angie. It wasn't a pillow snuggled so confidingly against his shoulder. It was Angie. And he was in her bed, just where he had no business being.

Travis forced his eyes open, stifling a groan when he saw the filtered sunlight that lit the room. He should have been out of there hours ago. He hadn't planned on falling asleep. But then it seemed as if, since meeting Angie, he was doing a lot of things he hadn't planned.

Somewhere in the house, a clock started to chime. Travis listened, counting the bells. Six o'clock. He had to get out of there. The last thing he needed was to run into Clay. There would be no explaining his presence in

Angie's room at this hour of the morning. Come to think of it, it would be pretty hard to explain at any hour.

Angie was lying against him, her head nestled on his shoulder, one arm across his chest. Her hair framed her face in soft golden curls. Her cheeks were flushed with sleep and her lips were slightly parted. She looked like a tousled angel—innocence and invitation in one soft package.

Travis lifted his hand, brushing a lock of hair away from her mouth. It curled around his fingers like the most delicate of shackles. He turned his hand, noticing how the pale gold of her hair contrasted with his tanned skin. Shadow and sun. His mouth twisted and he pulled his hand away, letting the curl drift back into place. He had to get out of there before he forgot just how big the gap between them really was.

Sometime during the night, Angie must have felt too warm because she'd pushed the light covers off, shoving them in his direction. Travis found his departure slowed by the need to untangle his legs from the discarded blankets. He'd just succeeded in freeing himself when he felt Angie's arm tighten across his chest.

"Where're you going?" Angie's voice was slurred with sleep.

"It's morning. I've got to go."

"Don't want you to." She sounded like a pouty child but there was nothing childlike in the way her hand slipped inside his shirt.

"Don't." He caught her hand, pressing it flat against his chest.

"Why not?" For the first time she opened her eyes and Travis felt his determination slipping a notch—several notches.

"I shouldn't be here," he told her, but his conviction was weakened by the fact that the arm against her back was shifting her subtly closer.

"I want you here." Her hand moved against his chest and his restraining hold eased, allowing her to curl her fingers against the hair-roughened skin.

"What about your brother?" Somehow, his hand had become entangled in her hair.

"I'm a big girl, Travis." Her eyes were midnight blue and held the promise of heaven on earth.

"So you are." The words were whispered against her mouth as he abandoned all thoughts of drawing away without kissing her. He had to taste her. Just one kiss, he promised his drowning sense of self-preservation. Just one kiss and then he'd go.

If her eyes promised heaven on earth, her mouth delivered on that promise. From the moment his lips touched hers, Travis knew he was lost. Or he would have known if he'd been able to think of anything beyond how right it felt to kiss her.

IT WAS SIMILAR TO WAKING to find herself in a wonderful dream, Angie thought. With Travis next to her, his kiss the first thing she felt, she couldn't imagine a better way to wake up. It should have felt strange, having a man in the bed where she'd slept alone most of her life. If it were any other man, maybe it would have. But not with Travis.

Her breath leaving her on a sigh, she shifted, turning farther into his arms. Her hand, still inside his shirt, slipped upward until her fingers slid into the silky hair at the base of his neck.

Her mouth parted, welcoming the warm thrust of his tongue as his hand flattened against her lower back, arching her closer as he deepened the kiss. The fire that seemed to always lay between them, banked and waiting, flared to life, and what had begun as a sleepy good-morning kiss was suddenly much more, something hot and powerful.

Travis's hand found its way beneath the T-shirt Angie wore, sliding up and down the warm skin of her back. When the elastic of her bra got in the way, he flicked the hooks open without a second's thought. He had to touch her and anything that got in the way was intolerable.

His hand traced the gentle curves of her back before settling on the indentation of her waist, then new territories beckoned and it was only a moment before his hand was drifting upward, finding its way beneath the loosened scrap of lace. Angie's breath caught as his fingers brushed the lower curve of her breast. If she had any thought of protest, it was burned away in an instant.

He cupped her breast boldly, his callused thumb brushing across her nipple. Angie felt his touch at her breast but she also felt the warmth of it spread through her body, turning her skin to fire.

She was hot silk in his hands, warm and yielding. She made him want to lose himself in the heat of her and yet he found the urge to protect her was as powerful as the need to take what she offered.

He dragged his mouth from hers, staring down into her flushed face. A sensuous angel. An impossible contradiction and yet it described her perfectly. She opened her eyes, staring up at him with a dazed look of passion that made his body tighten with aching need.

He wanted her. If he'd ever allowed himself to dream, she would have been the embodiment of those dreams.

A dream he didn't dare reach for.

If he let this continue, he could destroy the very things that made him want her most. Her sweet optimism, the way she looked at life through glasses tinted a pale shade of rose, her belief that life generally worked out for the best. He didn't share her feelings but that only made him want to protect her innocence even more.

Shadow and light. Angel and the bad man. Her belief against his cynicism. They were a study in contrasts. Two sides of a coin that could never meet. At least not without one destroying the other.

"Travis?" Angie touched her fingertips to the lines that had suddenly appeared beside his mouth. "What's wrong?"

He was.

But he couldn't give her that answer. She'd only argue, try to convince him otherwise. And at the moment he was perhaps a little too willing to be convinced.

"Nothing." He forced a twisted smile as he eased his hand from her breast. He pulled her shirt back down and rolled away from her to sit on the edge of the bed.

"Nothing?" He felt her sit up behind him and almost winced when she reached out to set her hand on his shoulder. "Then why..." She let the question trail off and Travis turned to look at her.

"Why did I stop?" He finished the thought for her.

Her cheeks were flushed but she nodded, her eyes steady on his. "That's right. Why did you? I mean, you must know that I... that I wanted you." She stumbled on the confession but managed to get the words out.

Travis stared at her, seeing the vulnerability in her eyes. He had only to say something flip and callous to devastate her, perhaps hurt her so badly that she'd stop thinking about him. He wouldn't have to worry about her turning up at his house or challenging him to a game of pool. She wouldn't come around to bandage his injuries and scold his housekeeping habits.

Just a few thoughtless words, delivered in just the right tone would end it all right there.

She drew her lower lip between her teeth in a gesture that showed how thin her casual front really was.

"This just isn't the time or place, Angel." He reached up to rub his thumb across the lip she'd been worrying. "If your brother finds me here, he's likely to shoot first and ask for an explanation much later."

"Clay isn't my keeper," she said hotly.

"No. But he's your brother and he worries about you." His mouth twisted in a rueful smile. "To tell the truth, if I were in his shoes, I'd feel the same way about you."

"I wish the two of you would stop talking like you're Charles Manson," she said. "So far, I've seen you do all sorts of terrible things, like rescuing me from a bunch of thugs and giving Mrs. Aggretti a job and driving me home in the rain. Heavens, who knows what dreadful crime you may commit next."

There was a certain anger in her eyes. Anger *for* him, not *at* him. Travis felt something shift inside, as if a long-held wall were in danger of cracking. In all his life, he'd never had anyone so unhesitatingly take his side. His parents had rarely noticed him enough to care whether he *had* a side to take and his grandfather had been of the guilty-until-proven-innocent school, especially when it came to the grandson he neither wanted nor understood.

But it didn't change anything. It didn't change what he was and it didn't change the potential for hurting her.

"You don't know me, Angel. You don't know what I'm capable of."

She reached up to catch his hand, pressing it to her cheek. "I know you're a good man, Travis, whether you believe it or not."

"I'm not totally without redeeming value but I don't think very many people have seen fit to call me a 'good' man," he said without rancor.

Shaking his head, he drew his hand out of her hold. "You're seeing what you want to see," he said as he rose. "And that's not necessarily reality."

"Then show me the reality," she said. "Show me why I shouldn't trust you. Show me why you're so sure you're bad for me. And if you can't show me, then I don't want to hear about it anymore."

Travis turned to look down at her. "Now I see how you keep your patients in line. You sound like a nanny I had when I was eight. I was scared to death of her. But you're much prettier than she was." He reached out and brushed her sleep-tousled hair back from her face. "I've got to go."

He touched his fingers to her mouth, still swollen from his kisses, then turned and walked away, knowing that if he lingered another minute he wouldn't leave at all. He refused to look back at her as he opened the door, not wanting to test his resolve. He might not have convinced her to stay away from him but at least he'd managed to walk out of there without taking advantage of her misplaced faith in him. He pulled open the door.

And found himself looking into Clay's shocked eyes.

The two of them stared at each other. For the space of a heartbeat, neither moved, both too stunned by the unexpected encounter to react. Clay recovered first, his look of shock turning to one of burning anger in the blink of an eye.

Travis had only an instant to see Clay's raised hand. He jerked his head back and the blow that should have dropped him in his tracks landed with much less force than intended. Still, it was enough to send him stumbling back against the door he hadn't had a chance to close. It flew open, revealing Angie still sitting in the middle of her rumpled bed, the imprint of two heads plain to see on the pillows.

"You sonofabitch!" Clay threw another punch, which Travis dodged.

"Cool it, man. This isn't what it looks like." Travis backed away, raising his hands in a gesture intended to calm. It didn't have any visible effect on the other man.

"You miserable, stinking scum!" Clay drew back his fist but Angie was suddenly between them.

"Stop it!"

"Don't!" Travis grabbed her by the shoulders and thrust her out of the way, afraid that Clay might not be able to pull his punch in time to avoid hitting her.

Clay's fist skimmed through the air, mere inches from where she'd been and Travis felt his heart nearly stop when he saw how close she'd come to being hurt.

"You stupid fool!" His determination to remain passive vanished in a blaze of primal anger. "Do you know what you almost did?"

"What *I* almost did?" Clay had recovered from the shock of narrowly missing his sister and he stepped forward to meet Travis's furious look. "Who the hell are you to be telling me what *I* almost did?"

"Stop it! Both of you, just stop it right now." Angie thrust herself between the two of them again, her usually gentle features hard with anger. "If either of you throws another punch, I swear I'm going to get a gun and shoot the pair of you. Do you hear me?"

She looked at both of them, letting them see the full force of the anger in her eyes.

"I hear you," Clay said sullenly. Travis only shrugged but Angie took that as agreement.

"What on earth are you doing, Clay?" Since her brother had started the fight, he bore the full brunt of her fury.

"What the hell is *he* doing?" Clay demanded, gesturing to Travis.

"That's none of your business," she told him sharply.

"None of my business?" He gave her an incredulous look. "I'm your brother."

"My brother. *Not* my keeper."

"Look, this isn't what it looks like," Travis interjected.

"We don't owe him an explanation," Angie said but he ignored the protest.

"Nothing happened last night. She'd had too much to drink so I brought her home and carried her up to bed." He dabbed at his bleeding lip with the back of his hand. "I fell asleep. End of story."

"End of story?" Clay's mood showed no sign of lightening. "I find you walking out of my sister's bedroom at six o'clock in the morning and I'm supposed to buy that you just *fell asleep?*" His tone expressed his disbelief and Travis's back stiffened.

"That's all the explanation you're getting," he said flatly. "Take it or leave it."

"You forget. I know you, Morgan." He stabbed a finger in the other man's direction. "And I don't trust you any farther than I could throw you. Not when it comes to my sister."

"Stop it!" Angie slapped his hand down. "I'm not invisible here. And I'm not a child. The bottom line,

Clay, is that it doesn't matter whether you believe him or not. If I want to sleep with Travis or any other man, it's none of your business.''

"But Angie, he's—"

"I don't want to hear it." She interrupted him with a quick, slashing motion of her hand. "I don't want to hear another word about it."

She turned to Travis, her eyes stormy blue with emotion. "I think it might be better if you left."

Travis looked from her to Clay, his eyes pale green and as cold as ice. He wiped the last of the blood from his split lip and nodded slowly.

"Sure, Angel." He reached out to cup his hand around the back of her neck and bent to kiss her without haste. It was less a kiss of passion than a staking of territory. It was meant as a clear message to Clay, one that couldn't be mistaken.

NEITHER ANGIE NOR CLAY spoke until they heard the sound of the front door closing quietly behind Travis.

"Angie, how..."

"I don't want to hear it, Clay." She cut him off ruthlessly. "I don't want to hear another word about his being a bad man. I don't want to hear anything from you but an apology."

"An apology!" He stared at her in disbelief. "You've got to be kidding. You want me to apologize? For what?"

"For acting like an ape," she snapped. Angie rubbed her fingers over her forehead, aware that a somewhat violent ache was starting just above her eyes.

"I reacted like any man would have. Any man who found someone leaving his sister's bedroom at six o'clock in the morning. And what did he mean when he said you'd had too much to drink?"

"Exactly what it sounds like," she shot back, refusing to give an inch. "I was drunk and he brought me home and carried me up to bed. Truly villainous behavior." She sneered.

"Considering that he stayed in your bed, I hardly think it earns him a nomination for sainthood. Unless taking advantage of a woman who's had too much to drink has suddenly become a good deed."

"I *asked* him to stay!" Angie closed her eyes in pain as the sound of her own raised voice echoed inside her head like a trumpet blast in a barrel. When she opened them again, it was to find her brother staring at her in shocked disbelief.

"You *asked* him to stay?"

"Yes. And it wasn't my idea that he left when he did," she admitted. "I'm sorry if that shocks you, Clay, but you've got to get used to the idea that I'm a grown woman. And who I choose to sleep with is none of your business."

"Angie, you can't—"

"I can do anything I want," she said, interrupting him. "Back off, Clay. I mean it."

"What the hell's gotten into you." He exploded. "You barely know this man and you're talking about sleeping with him. What kind of hold does he have over you?"

"You make it sound like he's Svengali and I'm some poor country maiden under his spell." Angie thrust her sleep-tangled hair back from her face and glared at him. "He's exciting."

"So is bungee jumping," he snapped. "And it's safer."

"Maybe I'll try that next week."

They faced each other, exchanging glare for glare. It was Clay who broke the silence first.

"I've told you he's dangerous, Angie. Isn't that enough?" His expression had gone from anger to something very close to pleading.

"Maybe I *like* it that he's dangerous," she said slowly. "Maybe I like it that he's different from anyone I've ever known." She wished she understood it better herself so that she could try to make Clay understand.

"You're not some foolish teenager whose head is turned by every punk in a black leather jacket. Hell, you weren't turned on by that kind of guy when you *were* a teenager," he said, exasperated.

"Travis isn't a punk, Clay. If you weren't so determined to dislike him, maybe you'd be able to see that."

"What I see is that he blows back into town with no visible means of support and starts hitting on my sister." He exploded, losing his temper again. "And she's stupid enough to fall for that whole 'bad boy' image. I thought you were smarter than that, Angie."

"Well, I'm sorry to disappoint you," she said, sarcasm making the apology sound less than sincere. "But this is *my* life and I'm old enough to live it as I choose. Now butt out and go away."

"But—"

"Out."

Clay looked at her, gauging her determination. Angie met his eyes, hoping she didn't look as fragile as she was starting to feel. Not only was her head pounding, but her stomach was beginning to send messages that suggested it was highly displeased with last night's excesses.

"All right," he said at last. "But this discussion isn't over."

"Fine." Angie nodded and then had to close her eyes as the movement set the room swirling around her. She didn't open them again until she heard the door close behind her brother.

Blessedly alone, she groped her way to the bed and sank onto the edge of it. The pounding in her head eased somewhat once she was off her feet.

God, what a morning. How to go from dream to nightmare in ten minutes or less, she thought ruefully. Waking in Travis's arms had been wonderful. Having Clay start a fight with him had been dreadful.

Angie smoothed her hand over the pillow Travis had used, her expression softening. Leaning down, she drew in a deep breath, inhaling the faint, masculine scent that lingered on the pillowcase. If she closed her eyes, it was almost similar to having him there.

Heavens, listen to the way she was thinking. She sounded like a love-struck teenager.

Wasn't that what she was?

Angie sat bolt upright as the small voice echoed in her mind. Ignoring the fact that the abrupt movement renewed the pounding in her head, she stared at her reflection in the dresser mirror across the room. Her eyes were rounded with shock and her pallor was caused by more than the vague hangover that threatened.

Love struck? Her? With Travis?

The disjointed questions popped into her head at random. The answers were prompt and consistent. Yes. Yes. And yes.

"My God. I'm in love with him." The words were a whisper, hardly audible and yet seeming to echo like a shout.

It wasn't possible. She hardly knew him. She was too sensible to fall in love with a man she hardly knew.

That was the sort of behavior to be expected from girls with more hair than sense. And even as a girl, she hadn't been the sort to get crushes and fancy herself in love with every handsome boy who came around.

She'd never have imagined herself falling in love with a man like Travis. All dark and dangerous, full of shadows and secrets.

But all the logic in the world wouldn't change the facts. She'd fallen in love with Travis Morgan. She was in love with a man about whom she knew next to nothing. She didn't even know what he did for a living, for God's sake.

Did it matter?

Still staring at her reflection, she picked up his pillow and hugged it to her chest. Did anything matter except that her heart beat faster when he was in the room? Or that she'd never felt so alive in her entire life as she had since meeting him?

She was in love. This time, she let the idea sink in. Happiness bubbled up inside her, defying the grumbling threat of a hangover.

She, Angie Brady, was in love with Travis Morgan.

She grinned at her reflection. She wanted to shout it to the world. She wanted to find Travis and throw her arms around him and tell him that she loved him.

Her smile faded. Would Travis even want to hear such a confession? It would be foolish to assume that, just because she'd realized she was in love with him, Travis felt the same way about her.

But he had to love her, she argued passionately. It wasn't possible to love someone so much and not have that love returned. Except she knew it *was* possible. Her father had loved her mother deeply and yet Evelyn Brady had had no qualms about walking out on him and their two children. Because he was boring, she'd told him with blunt cruelty.

Angie wrapped her hands around her upper arms, unconsciously hugging herself as if she could keep the cold chill of reality from intruding on her newly discovered emotions.

Just because her mother hadn't loved her father—or her children—didn't mean that Travis wouldn't love her. He *wanted* her—that much she could be sure of. Remembering the taut length of his body against hers just a short while ago in this very bed, Angie felt her confidence take a subtle swing upward.

They definitely shared that elusive thing called chemistry. Perhaps, in that chemistry, lay the seeds of an enduring relationship. It was up to her to cultivate that seed, to give it a chance to grow.

She lay back on the bed, pressing her cheek to the pillow Travis had used, her eyes both dreamy and determined. She had a pretty good idea of where to start her gardening efforts.

Chapter Eight

Travis leaned his shoulder against the warped door that led from the garage to the kitchen. It yielded grudgingly to a superior force, giving in with a squeal of hinges that suggested it might not always be so easily conquered.

He'd thought about oiling the hinges but they were as good a burglar alarm as anything he could buy. Certainly no one was going to be sneaking up on him through *this* door.

The rest of the house had its own defenses. Nothing that would seem at all out of the ordinary to a casual thief but enough to provide Travis with a warning of any intrusion, whether he was home or not.

Entering the kitchen, he automatically stepped over the buckled piece of linoleum and set a small sack of groceries on the scuffed counter. He shrugged out of his leather jacket and tossed it onto a chair before opening the refrigerator and pulling out a cold beer.

Twisting off the top, he took a swallow, letting the icy liquid flow slowly down his throat.

The unusually cool, damp spring had disappeared overnight, burned away by the heat wave that announced summer's arrival. It was after nine in the evening and the temperature outside still hovered in the upper seventies. Inside the old house it was closer to eighty-five. The sun had had all day to beat down on the sagging roof. The fact that the windows were painted shut meant that not so much as a breath of air stirred in the dim rooms.

Sipping the beer, Travis emptied the sack of groceries, throwing the perishables into the refrigerator and leaving everything else sitting on the counters to be put away when the temperature dropped, maybe sometime in October.

He moved into the living room, carrying the bottle in one hand. He flicked on one lamp. The sixty-watt bulb banished only the deepest shadows but the gloom suited his mood. There was a fan in the living room and he turned it on. It didn't accomplish much beyond stirring the hot air around but it was enough to give the illusion of cooling.

Sinking into the one chair in the house that offered reasonable comfort—a black leather armchair that had seen better days—he stretched his long legs out in front of him and leaned his head back against the cracked leather. With the cold beer in his hand and the soft whir of the fan for company, he closed his eyes and tried to make his mind as blank as possible.

Immediately a pair of summer-sky-blue eyes appeared in front of him. Warm and soft and full of passion, they beckoned to him, just as her soft mouth did. He could almost taste that mouth, almost feel that hunger in her, a hunger that had nearly matched his own. And her soft, wildflower scent, the feel of her skin beneath his hands...

"Dammit!" His eyes flew open and he sat bolt upright in the chair, his hand clenched around the beer bottle. So much for relaxing. His body was as taut as a bow string.

"Idiot," he muttered as he got up. What was wrong with him, sitting here thinking about a woman and getting aroused like some randy teenager?

But not just any woman, he admitted reluctantly. And that was the heart of the problem. Unlike the teenager he'd compared himself to, he wasn't interested in any blonde with staples in her belly. He would have preferred that. Good old-fashioned, generic lust was easy enough to ignore.

What bothered him was that this was a very specific blonde that had him hard and aching. And he wasn't feeling anything as simple as lust, either. He wanted her but there was more to it than that.

And *that* was the problem.

He swigged down the last of the beer, already slightly warm, and then stalked into the kitchen for another. But the fresh, ice-cold brew did little to cool his heated thoughts. Nor did it numb his thinking to the point where he could convince himself that Angie Brady meant nothing more to him than a pleasant diversion.

The fact was he liked her. He scowled at the chipped enamel on the refrigerator door. He *cared* about her, he thought, forcing himself to be honest. He was a hairbreadth away from falling in love with her, he admitted bleakly, forcing himself to complete honesty.

Disaster. That was what it would be. Emotional suicide. For both of them. Unless he read her wrong, Angie had just about convinced herself that she was in love with him. And remembering the look in her eyes this morning, he wasn't sure "just about" was an accurate description anymore.

He wandered back into the living room, the beer forgotten in his hand. He'd told himself that she wouldn't get hurt. He was no longer at all sure that was true. If he broke it off now, she was going to be hurt. If he broke it off later, she was going to be hurt.

And if he didn't break it off?

The thought slipped in unbidden and Travis's fingers clenched around the bottle. If he didn't break it off, then he was the one who would end up paying the price. Sooner or later, Angie would figure out that he wasn't the man she'd imagined him to be and those beautiful blue eyes would look at him with the same disappointment he'd seen in his parents. Or the look of dislike with which his grandfather had always regarded him.

He took a swallow of beer, wishing it were something stronger. Something that might burn away the old memories. Memories he'd thought he put behind him a long time ago. But then Angie had a tendency to make him think of things he hadn't thought of in a long time. Things such as white picket fences and family ties. The sort of things he'd long since decided were not for him.

Travis sighed and lifted the bottle to press it against his forehead, letting the cool glass cool his skin. Too bad it couldn't do as much to cool his overheated imagination. Even knowing how foolish it was, he couldn't stop thinking about the way Angie had looked this morning, the way she'd felt in his arms.

There was no doubt about it: He had to put some distance between them. For his sake, as well as hers. Nothing but trouble could come of the two of them.

It was almost a relief when someone knocked on the door. In this neighborhood, it would likely mean trouble, but at least it was a distraction. Eager as he was for that, he didn't ignore common sense. He didn't stand right in front of the door; he approached it from the side instead.

"Yeah?" His tone was not particularly welcoming, nor was the hand that rested on the gun tucked against the small of his back.

"Travis?"

Angie.

Travis let his hand drop from the gun. What was she doing here? Had thinking about her been enough to conjure her up? The way things had been going lately, he was willing to believe it. He pulled the gun out of the waistband of his pants and put it out of reach. Then, unable to behave as reluctantly as he ought to, he pulled open the door.

In contrast to the dimly lit room, the porch was flooded with light from the new fixture Travis had put up not long after he rented the place. It sometimes paid to have a clear view of one's visitors.

The light shone off Angie's hair, turning it to pure gold.

"Hi."

"Hi." Travis cleared his throat, which seemed suddenly tight. "What are you doing here?"

"Glad to see you, too," she said with an uncertain laugh.

"Sorry." He thrust his fingers through his hair and half smiled. "I think the heat melted my brain. Come in."

He stepped back to allow her in and then shut the door behind her. Turning to look at her, he noticed that the dingy room seemed suddenly brighter, as if she carried sunshine inside.

"It is hot, isn't it?" she said.

"Yeah. It's hot." He was hardly conscious of what he was saying. He couldn't take his eyes off the bare skin of her shoulders. Talk about a melted brain. Her dress was enough to cause a permanent meltdown.

Her shoulders were completely bare except for a pair of thin straps that held up the bodice. Peacock-blue cotton molded her breasts and clung to her waist before falling in graceful folds to just above her knees. When she half turned to set her purse on the sofa, Travis could see that the thin straps crossed in the middle of her back. And that was all that covered her back.

His fingers slowly curled into the palms of his hands. He knew from personal experience just how that length of exposed skin felt. And this time, there was no annoying strap to dispose of, just that wonderful expanse of bare skin.

Her hair was caught up on top of her head in one of those soft buns that made a woman look as if she'd just stepped out of the bath and made a man think all sorts of things he shouldn't.

He swallowed hard and closed his eyes for a moment, reminding himself that, only moments ago, he'd decided that the best thing for all concerned was to keep his distance from Angie Brady. But she wasn't cooperating.

When he opened his eyes, she'd moved closer. She was close enough now that he could smell the light floral scent he'd come to associate with her, the scent that had haunted more than a few late-night dreams.

"What are you doing here?" He'd intended the question to sound harsh and unwelcoming. But even he could hear that it fell far short of the mark.

"I came to see you." Angie reached up to brush an invisible piece of lint from his shoulder. Travis felt the light touch burn through the fabric of his shirt. He cleared his throat.

"You shouldn't have come here, Angie."

"I keep thinking about this morning," she continued as if he hadn't spoken. "About how right it felt. Having you hold me, kiss me. Touch me." The last was hardly more than a whisper and the color in her cheeks told him that the bold words did not come as easily as she pretended.

It was that soft blush that kept him from saying something harsh, something guaranteed to put an end to this foolishness. Or that's what he told himself. That explanation grew a little thin however when he realized that he'd set his hands on her shoulders.

"Angel, this will never work." His words lacked conviction, especially since his thumbs were moving lightly over the fragile length of her collarbone.

"It seems to be working pretty well so far." She'd moved closer still and was looking up at him with those big blue eyes. What was it about her eyes that made it so difficult for him to keep track of what he should do?

"You can't use me as a club to beat your brother with," he told her.

"This has nothing to do with Clay. This is just you and me." Her fingers were working loose the buttons on his shirt.

He should stop her, of course. And he would. In just a minute.

"This isn't a good idea," he whispered huskily. His fingers had found the first of the pins that held her hair. Within seconds it was spilling over his hands, a waterfall of gold silk.

"I think it's a very good idea." She'd opened all the buttons she could reach before his belt blocked her path. She set her hands on his chest. Travis felt the light touch burn his skin.

She was so close, there was hardly room for a shadow between them. He could feel every breath she drew, see the tiny silver lines that spiraled through the blue of her eyes. Her scent filled his head.

He wanted her. God, how he wanted her. He'd never wanted—needed—anything in his life the way he needed Angie at this moment. She was all the things he wasn't. She completed everything he was missing. All the warmth and trust and faith he no longer felt.

His fingers slid through her hair, cupping her head, his eyes searching her face. Would it be so wrong to steal a little piece of her brightness? It was what she wanted. What he needed. Would it be so terrible to pretend? Just for a little while?

She stared into his eyes as his head lowered toward hers, her lashes lowering in the last half breath before his mouth touched hers. The battle was lost before it had begun. The moment he felt the soft warmth of her mouth, tasted her response, Travis knew there would be no turning back.

This was right, just as she'd said. This was what had to happen. Let the devil take tomorrow. Tonight he was going to taste heaven.

ANGIE HAD THOUGHT she knew what she was doing when she came here tonight. She thought it out calmly—or at least as calmly as she could when just the thought of Travis was enough to set her pulse pounding—and she made her decision. She expected some resistance on his part. He had this stupid idea that he wasn't good for her. But she'd been sure, with a deep feminine instinct she'd never realized she possessed, that he'd give in, his need as strong as hers.

What she hadn't expected was the way everything suddenly spiraled out of control the moment he touched her. It was as if she unleashed a fire, blazing hot and full of desire. There was no slow build to passion, no soft and gentle coaxing along pathways still relatively new to her.

Travis's mouth molded hers, his tongue skimming her lower lip and then plunging into her mouth as if he had to taste her or die. Angie's breath left her on a moan as impatient hands stripped the flimsy straps from her shoulders. The bodice dropped to her waist but there was no time to feel any uneasiness at being half nude in front of a man for the first time in her life because Travis's palms covered her breasts, his touch a sweet fire on her skin.

If she'd thought to feel a twinge of fear, he gave her no time for it. Her hands slid helplessly upward to cling to the strength of his shoulders as he wrapped his arms around her back, dragging her forward until they were molded together from shoulder to waist.

It wasn't until she sensed the light change against her closed eyelids that she realized he was carrying her. She opened her eyes as he set her on her feet next to a bed. His bedroom. His bed.

He released her long enough to wrench off the open shirt, tossing it behind him. Every nerve in his body screamed for him to tumble her onto the bed and ease the ache that had been gnawing at him since the day they met. But this wasn't some woman he'd picked up in a bar. This was Angie. And he was going to make it perfect for her.

"I think we need a light."

"No." Her protest was quick but not quick enough. With a click, the bedside lamp came on, banishing the shadows to the room's corners. Angie's hands came up as if to cover herself but he caught her wrists, holding her arms out to the side.

"Don't," he ordered softly. "I want to look at you."

His eyes skimmed her and the look in them made her forget her self-consciousness. The look said he found her beautiful.

"This morning, I tried to picture what you looked like. You felt so good, all soft and silky. But you're so much more beautiful than I even imagined." He released her hands, his own coming up to cup the soft mounds, his thumbs stroking over her nipples.

Angie's hands clenched in his hair as he bent and took one dusky peak into his mouth. Never in all her wildest dreams had she imagined a sensation so intense. Every nerve in her body responded to the gentle tugging of his mouth.

Just when she thought she might faint from the intensity of it, Travis lifted his head, his mouth coming down on hers as his hands slid around her back. Angie felt him working the zipper on her dress. An instant later, the light cotton started to slide down her hips. She felt a momentary panic at the thought of standing before him without even that dubious protection but it was too late. Her dress lay around her feet in a spill of peacock blue.

Travis lifted his head, his eyes catching hers in a look that made her forget her shyness, then he looked down at her nearly bare body. The hot weather had made hose unthinkable and she was clad in only a pair of scandalously small panties the same color as her discarded dress. The swatch of blue nylon and lace contrasted invitingly with her pale skin.

She saw Travis's reaction in the way the skin tightened over his cheekbones, heard it in the shallow breath he drew. And she felt more deeply feminine than she'd ever felt before. As if from outside herself, she saw her hand come out to rest on the heavy bulge at the front of his jeans. She felt him shudder in response to her light touch.

He dragged his eyes from her slender body and locked his gaze with hers as he reached for his belt. Angie let her hand drop back down to her side. The room was hot and still yet the rasp of his zipper brought goose bumps to life on her torso.

Without breaking his gaze from hers, Travis shoved his jeans and underwear down and off, kicking them aside impatiently. Angie automatically looked down. And forgot how to breathe.

She was a nurse, and as she'd told him, the male body held no surprises for her. Or so she'd thought until now. She was rapidly discovering that there was a wide gap between clinical knowledge and actually standing face-to-face with a naked, aroused man.

"Oh!" The small exclamation escaped her.

"Oh?" Travis's mouth quirked in a half smile. "Is that a good *oh* or a bad *oh?*"

"Just, oh." She dragged her gaze upward, not sure if it was nerves or lust that was making her knees weak.

"Oh." He repeated her exclamation softly, still smiling in that way that made her pulse beat much too fast.

He reached out to set one fingertip between her breasts and she was sure he must be able to feel the way her heart was pounding. He let the finger drift downward, pausing to explore the shallow indentation of her belly button before drifting to toy idly with the narrow elastic at the waist of her panties.

Angie felt her breath stop as he slid his fingers beneath the lace, easing it into the mat of golden curls. Her hands came up to grip his shoulders for support as he slipped his hand beneath the fragile layer of nylon.

"Travis." His name escaped her on a sigh as he found the damp heat of her.

"Angel." The endearment was almost a prayer as he lowered his mouth to hers.

She was all silk and fire. Satin skin and trembling warmth.

He lowered her to the bed, disposing of the last scrap of fabric that kept them apart. The day's heat that lingered in the room was nothing compared to the warmth they generated between them. Travis felt as if he couldn't get enough of her—her smell, her taste, the feel of her body against his.

And Angie seemed to feel the same way, clinging to him as if she'd never let him go. She responded to his every touch with trembling excitement; her caresses held a shy eagerness that was more arousing than the practiced touch of a courtesan.

When Travis was sure he couldn't wait another second to make her his, he stretched out one arm to the nightstand. He knocked the clock to the floor trying to find the packet he'd put there three days ago. At the time he'd recognized the irony of preparing for an event he'd sworn would never take place. Now, he was simply grateful for his own hypocrisy.

Angie flushed when she saw what he was doing but there was also a softness in her eyes that said she appreciated his thoughtfulness.

Her arms reached up to him, welcoming him into the warmth of her body. It was an invitation the hounds of hell could not have prevented Travis from accepting. His body throbbed with need. With a hunger like nothing he'd ever felt.

He tested himself against her, gauging her readiness. She moaned—a low, hungry sound in the back of her throat—and he knew he could wait no more.

He buried his hands in her hair, his mouth finding hers as he eased forward, savoring the slow sheathing of his aching need in her welcoming warmth. The last thing he'd expected was to feel the thin, unmistakable barrier that blocked his further entrance. His body went rigid with surprise and he jerked his head up, his eyes meeting hers.

"Don't go." Feeling him tense and seeing the shock in his eyes, Angie grabbed hold of his arms, her fingers digging into the corded muscles as she sought to hold him to her.

"God, Angie, why didn't you tell me?"

"It's not important," she said desperately, convinced that he was going to leave her, that she'd never find out what lay at the end of the path he'd swept her along. She lifted her legs, pressing her knees to his hips.

"Please, Travis." She had to find out what lay at the end of the journey they'd begun. She twisted restlessly beneath him. "Don't go."

"Angel." Travis lowered his mouth to hers. "I couldn't if I wanted to." He eased himself deeper, feeling the slow, grudging yielding. He swallowed her shallow gasp of discomfort as the barrier gave way, allowing him full access to the womanly depths of her.

He dragged his mouth from hers, drawing in deep breaths as he hammered his control into place. This was for her, he reminded himself. She had gifted him with something she could give but once and he would die before he'd do anything to make her regret that gift.

THE LAST THING Angie felt was regret. Wonder, pleasure, a deep sense of fulfillment, but not regret. She felt as if she'd been waiting all her life for this moment, for this man.

Her hands moved restlessly up and down the length of Travis's back, seeking something to cling to as he began to move over her. The fire he'd built inside her licked higher, threatening to blaze out of control. She wanted to let it burn, even as she half feared being consumed by the flames. She wanted... She needed... Her head twisted against the pillow, her body growing taut as she struggled to reach some goal she could almost see but didn't understand.

"Don't fight it so hard," Travis whispered against her ear. "Relax and let it happen."

She couldn't relax. And let what happen? If he didn't stop, she was going to break apart in a million pieces. And yet, she knew if he stopped now, she'd surely die. It was so close. So very, very close.

Her hands clung to his shoulders as she felt him lift himself away from her. For a moment, she thought he was leaving her and she felt a surge of panic. He couldn't go, not until she found...not until she knew...

And then suddenly she was spinning directly into the heart of the fire. Only the fire was within her, consuming her, melting her.

Travis watched the heat run up under her skin as the climax took her. Her eyes flew wide, staring up at him with shocked wonder as her body went taut. He wanted to savor her fulfillment, to take her even farther but the delicate contractions inside her rippled over him, tumbling him headlong into the fire they'd built together.

IT WAS A LONG TIME before he gathered the strength to move off of her. She murmured a protest and tightened her arms around him.

"I'll squash you," he said, his voice husky.

"I don't care. Don't go."

"I'm not going far." He settled beside her, sliding one arm under her to pull her close.

Angie snuggled her head into his shoulder as if she'd been sleeping that way for years. Travis stroked his hand up and down her damp back. He felt deeply relaxed, a rare experience in his life. It was more than just sating the sexual hunger he'd felt since meeting Angie. It went deeper than that, as if he'd found a part of himself he hadn't even known was missing.

"You should have told me," he said.

"Then you wouldn't have made love to me." She didn't pretend not to know what he was talking about. "You'd have gone all noble on me." She tilted her head to look up at him, her eyes full of soft humor and Travis found himself wanting her all over again.

"I wouldn't be too sure of that," he admitted slowly. He reached out to stroke a damp curl back from her forehead. "I think lust might have won out over nobility."

"Lust?" She rolled onto her stomach and put her hand flat on his chest, setting her chin on that prop. "Lust?" She grinned. "I like the sound of that."

"Why?" He couldn't resist the urge to run his fingers through the tangled silk of her hair.

"Because it makes it sound as if you couldn't resist me."

"Obviously I couldn't."

"I knew you wouldn't be able to." She curled the fingers of her free hand into the mat of dark blond hair on his chest.

"You knew that, did you?"

"Of course. Didn't you know I'm irresistible?" She batted her lashes at him in a fair imitation of a femme fatale.

"I'm beginning to get that impression," he said dryly.

He couldn't ever remember having a conversation like this after sex. Generally he wanted only to fall asleep. But then, this was the first time he'd found himself in bed with Angie, and around her, nothing seemed to be as it usually was.

Angie laid her head flat against his chest, listening to the steady beat of his heart. She could feel that beat beneath her palm, too, strong and even. She closed her eyes and combed her fingers through the mat of hair on his chest.

She felt completed in a way she'd never known before, as if a part of her that had been missing was now found. Her body was at once completely relaxed and more alive than ever before.

When she'd decided to come here and seduce Travis, she'd had a few doubts, wondering if she were making the right choice. Now it was hard to remember why she'd even wondered. Her mouth curved in a soft, secretive smile. It had been worth waiting to find out what all the hoopla was about. It had been more than worth waiting.

Travis tilted his head to look at Angie's face. She'd fallen asleep, he realized. Sprawled across his chest like a tired kitten, she was sound asleep. His mouth relaxed in a smile that would have surprised quite a few people who thought they knew him. It would have surprised him, if he'd happened to look in a mirror. Tenderness was not an emotion he generally connected with himself.

Damn, but she was beautiful. And she was his.

His arm tightened around her as he shifted her to a more comfortable position against his shoulder. She muttered something unintelligible and frowned slightly before nuzzling her face into his skin and throwing one arm across his chest.

His. Travis looked at her sleeping face and allowed a wave of purely masculine possessiveness to wash over him. Right or wrong, she belonged to him in a way no other woman ever had. In a way she could never belong to another man. No matter what happened in the future, there'd be no forgetting this night for either of them.

As if he could ever forget anything about her, he thought. What was it about her that made him feel things he'd never felt before? Reminded him of old dreams he'd thought long gone? She almost made him believe in the future again.

He rested his cheek against her head. This couldn't last, of course. Sooner or later, something would happen and she'd see him as he really was. Travis closed his eyes, blocking out the thought. He'd deal with that when the time came. But he didn't want to think about it now.

He didn't want to think about anything now except how right she felt in his arms. In his bed. He'd dared to love an angel, he thought, just on the edge of sleep. There'd be a price to pay, but for the moment, he was just going to savor the miracle of it.

Chapter Nine

"Let me drive you home."

"And have Clay shoot you on the doorstep?" Angie was smiling as she shook her head. "I'll be fine. Have you seen my other shoe?"

Travis glanced around the bedroom and lifted his bare shoulders in a shrug. "I wasn't particularly interested in your shoes earlier."

"Neither was I," she acknowledged, flushing lightly as she remembered just how little interest she'd had in anything but him. Shoes had been the least of her concerns.

She had to admit she didn't care much about finding them now. Travis was standing at the foot of the bed, wearing a pair of jeans that rode low on his hips. They were zipped but not buttoned and Angie curled her fingers into her palm against the urge to lower that zipper.

"If you keep looking at me like that, you're never going to get a chance to find your shoes."

The husky threat jerked her eyes to his face and the way he was looking at her made her flush deepen. It promised all sorts of things, promises she was tempted to take up. With an effort she forced her eyes away from the temptation.

"I've got to go to work," she said, the reminder as much for herself as for him.

"Then I guess you're going to need your shoes."

The lost shoe was finally located in the living room. It must have fallen off when he picked her up to carry her into the bedroom, she thought. She had to force her mind away from that line of thinking before she decided that going to work wasn't important.

"I'll follow you home." Travis appeared in the bedroom doorway, shrugging into a shirt.

"That's not necessary."

"I don't want you driving home alone at this hour of the morning."

"Travis, it's almost dawn. Even the bad guys are asleep by now. Besides, I'm going to be in my car and I'll lock the doors."

"I'll follow you home." There was no arguing with the flat statement but Angie tried anyway.

"It's really not . . ."

"Necessary," Travis finished for her. He crossed the few feet that separated them and stopped in front of her. Brushing his fingers across her cheek, he looked down at her, his eyes gray green in the dimly lit room. "I'll follow you home," he said softly.

"Okay." She'd have agreed to almost anything he said as long as he was standing so close and looking at her that way. She turned her face into his hand, her eyes half closing as his thumb brushed over her lower lip.

"You know I'm beginning to think you're not an angel," he said huskily.

"I never said I was." Her teeth nibbled his thumb before her tongue came out to taste him. Angie felt a surge of purely feminine satisfaction at the way his eyes darkened to deep green as he watched her. He drew his hand away from her mouth, shifting it to cup the back of her neck.

"I think you're a witch," he whispered just before his mouth touched hers.

Angie melted into him, her arms coming up to circle his neck, her body pliant against his. As she'd already discovered, her self-control faded at his lightest touch. She instantly forgot about going home. If he'd picked her up and carried her back to bed, she wouldn't have offered a word of protest.

"I thought you had to go home and change for work," he murmured against her ear.

"I could call in sick," she said, feeling a delicious shiver work its way up her spine when his teeth caught her earlobe and bit gently.

"No." She could feel the effort it cost him to straighten and step away from her. Even then, he couldn't prevent his fingers from lingering in her hair. "You should get home. Your brother will be worried sick if he finds out you didn't come home last night. Chances are, this is the first place he'll look."

"I'm a little too old to be reporting in to Clay," Angie told him, her mouth tightening in annoyance. "He's going to have to get used to it because this isn't going to be the last time I spend the night with you."

She caught her breath as she realized what she'd said. The flush that rose in her cheeks was dark and painful.

"Oh, God. That sounded so presumptuous." She pressed her hands to her hot cheeks. "I didn't mean to assume... I mean, if you didn't want..."

"I want." Travis reached out and pulled her into his arms.

Angie felt the solid beat of his heart beneath her ear and felt as if she'd come home. The words "I love you" trembled on the tip of her tongue. But now was not the time. She knew instinctively that it would be a mistake to tell him how she felt now.

"You'd better get going," Travis said, after a moment, releasing her with obvious reluctance.

Angie hugged that reluctance to her as she drove home. That, and the presence of the motorcycle's headlight behind her. The eastern sky was just starting to show a hint of gray when she pulled into the driveway.

Travis had slowed the motorcycle to a stop in the street and she knew he was waiting to make sure that she got into the house safely. Once she had the front door open, she waved her arm to let him know she was safe. He lifted his hand in acknowledgement and then lifted his foot off the pavement and sent the motorcycle off down the street, the engine's roar loud in the quiet neighborhood.

Angie sneaked up the stairs to her room, glad that Clay's room was at the back of the house, where he was unlikely to have heard the bike. Closing the door of her room behind her, she wrapped her arms around her waist and leaned back against it, letting the night's memories wash over her.

Travis cared. Oh, he wasn't ready to admit it yet but she could see it in his eyes when he looked at her. And she'd felt it in his touch last night. She wasn't naive enough to think that he loved her just because he'd made love to her. But there'd been more than passion in his touch. There'd been a tenderness there, a concern that put her needs above his own. A man didn't treat a woman with such care if he didn't feel something more than simple desire for her.

Angie pushed away from the door and drifted over to the window. Opening the curtains, she stared out at the dawn just breaking over the horizon. She felt as fresh and new and full of hope as the new day.

There were still barriers between them, she thought, forcing herself to be realistic. Something inside Travis was fighting the feelings growing between them. She didn't know what it was, why he was so determined to keep her at a distance. Even after last night, she'd felt him putting up walls, trying to keep her from getting too close.

He wanted her—that much he'd been forced to admit. And he cared about her—that much she'd seen in his eyes. For now, it was enough.

TRAVIS PUSHED open the clinic door and stepped inside. There were three people in the waiting room: a mother with a fussy toddler and an old man who sat staring at the wall opposite with blank eyes.

"I need your name and the reason for your visit."

Travis turned to look at the woman who sat behind the scarred counter that served as an admittance desk. She was a heavy-set redhead in her late thirties, wearing a hot pink blouse that clashed so magnificently with her hair it was almost a fashion statement. She looked at him with curiosity, her dark eyes skimming his tall figure as if wondering what injury or illness had brought him to the Fair Street Clinic.

"I'm here to see Angie Brady," he said.

"She's with a patient." The curiosity had turned to speculation and Travis shifted uneasily beneath the questions in her eyes.

"Will she be long?"

"Probably not. I could tell her you're here, if you want."

"I'd appreciate that. Just tell her it's Travis."

"Travis." The woman repeated his name slowly, rolling it on her tongue as if trying to extract more information from that one meager tidbit.

"Anything else I should tell her?" she asked hopefully.

"No." He added nothing to the flat word and after a moment, she heaved herself up from the stool. "You can wait in the waiting room, if you like. That's what it's there for." She grinned at him, revealing a set of perfect teeth.

Judging by her reaction, there obviously weren't many men who came around asking for Angie. He tried not to feel a twinge of pleasure at the thought.

Travis glanced at the small waiting room to find that the young woman was looking at him, ignoring the child who was tugging on her skirt and whining about wanting a cookie. The old man had also shifted his attention from the empty wall to Travis, making him feel like an exhibit at the zoo.

He turned away from their curious looks, pretending enormous interest in a poster that pointed out the health hazards of cigarette smoking. Next to that was a poster detailing the terrible things that could happen when you took drugs. He wondered if the message had any impact on the kids it was intended to reach. He certainly hadn't seen much evidence that it did. And Shearson's business didn't show any signs of slowing.

"Angie said to tell you she'd be just a couple of minutes." The receptionist's words interrupted his thinking and Travis turned to look at her.

"Thanks." Travis glanced at the waiting room and found he was still the main object of interest. "Tell her I'll wait outside, would you?"

The receptionist had followed his glance and now her eyes came back to him. She grinned. "We don't get many healthy specimens in here," she offered, by way of explanation.

"Yeah, well, I'm starting to feel like a bug under a microscope. I'll wait outside."

"I'll tell Angie."

Travis nodded his thanks and escaped outside. He preferred dealing with the heat reflected off the pavement to facing the curious stares inside. He found a shady spot near the corner of the building and settled himself on the waist-high retaining wall that marked that edge of the property.

His position allowed him to see without being easily seen. He shouldn't have come here, he thought, glancing around uncomfortably. His relationship with Angie wasn't something he wanted made known, not to Shearson or to the police. And showing up at the clinic to see her was probably a dumb move. But then, he seemed to be doing a lot of dumb things these days.

He reached into his pocket for a stick of gum, folding it into his mouth. It had only been a few hours since he followed Angie home but he'd been thinking about when he'd see her again from the moment she stepped out of his sight.

Last night had been...extraordinary. Angie had been everything he'd fantasized she would be—and more. She'd given herself to him without hesitation, offering herself with a trust that was strangely erotic. He found himself wanting to take everything she offered, yet wanting to protect her from the possible consequences of her generosity. He'd done more of the former than the latter, he admitted.

Yet he couldn't find it in him to regret the night they'd spent together. He'd done exactly what he'd sworn not to: he'd gotten involved with Angie. But he just couldn't manage to regret one of the best nights of his life.

And he didn't think Angie had any regrets, either. There was an undeniable surge of male satisfaction in remembering the soft look in her eyes after they'd made love—the look of a woman who'd been thoroughly pleasured.

Travis shifted uncomfortably and turned his thoughts in less erotic directions. He stared down at the foil gum wrapper that his fingers had been absently folding into a neat little square and tried to picture where he and Angie were going to go from here.

God, listen to him. He was actually thinking in terms of having some kind of future with this woman. For the first time since he was a teenager, he was actually thinking it might be possible to build something lasting with another person.

"What the hell are you doing here?"

The sharp question jerked Travis out of his half-formed imaginings. He lifted his head to find Clay standing in front of him, his stocky body tense, feet braced apart as if for a fight.

"I'm waiting for Angie."

Travis slipped the wrapper into his pocket but didn't stand up. It was obvious that Clay would like nothing better than to punch him in the mouth again. Ordinarily Travis would have been happy to oblige, but brawling in a parking lot wasn't going to do anybody any good and it would upset Angie.

"I told you to stay away from her," Clay said.

"I think Angie's old enough to make her own decisions."

"Not about this." Clay stared at him, worry and anger darkening his eyes. "Dammit, Morgan! I don't want to see her hurt."

"Neither do I."

"You're not doing a whole hell of a lot to prevent it. I pulled your file," he said baldly.

Travis stiffened, his eyes suddenly more gray than green. "So?"

"So, I know what you're into. I know exactly what you're doing. And I know my sister is going to get badly hurt when you get yourself arrested. Or killed." He added the last deliberately, the words a warning. "And if you manage to avoid both of those, you're going to leave without a backward glance when you've got what you want."

"Maybe I'm starting to think about settling down," Travis said slowly, only then realizing how much he wanted to believe it was possible.

"You?" Clay's tone was scornful. "You're not the type. You're going to spend your life getting into trouble, the way you always have."

"A man can change."

"Some men. But not you. You're born to trouble, Morgan. You and I both know it. I don't know where this sudden urge for roots came from but I don't want you testing the idea out on my sister. If you care for her at all, even the smallest amount, leave her alone."

"I've never played games with anyone who didn't know the score."

"Angie doesn't know the score," Clay snapped. "And I don't want her learning it from you."

"It's a little late for that," Travis muttered.

"What's that supposed to mean?" Clay fairly bristled with hostility.

They faced each other, only a breath away from a full-blown brawl. One wrong word and Clay was going to go for his throat. Travis reminded himself of how much it would upset Angie to find him fighting with her brother and willed the tension from his shoulders.

"It means that Angie is a grown woman, not a child, and you've got to let her make her own mistakes."

"A mistake is one thing but she's walking right into a disaster."

"You make me sound like the Titanic," Travis said, trying to lighten the atmosphere. But Clay wasn't about to be humored out of his mood.

"What about Shearson? What about your involvement with him? Have you considered that Angie could get caught in the crossfire?"

Travis's expression tightened as Clay's words touched a sore spot. "I guess that you know as well as I do that Shearson's in Tahiti until the end of the week. There's not a damn thing going to happen until he gets back."

"And when he gets back?" Clay pressed. "What about Angie, then?"

"I'll make sure she's out of the picture," Travis said shortly.

"Have you told her what you're doing?"

"I haven't lied to her," Travis said evasively.

"Stay away from her," Clay said again, his eyes bright blue and determined. "I won't have her hurt because you've made a mess of your life."

"I'm not going to hurt her, dammit!" Even as he made the promise, Travis wondered if he was going to be able to keep it.

"If you hurt her, I'm going to personally tear you limb from limb." Clay's voice was low and hard.

Their eyes met, green crossing blue in a silent battle that neither could win. It occurred to Travis that there was something ironic in the fact that they were practically at each other's throats although they shared the same goal, which was simply to protect Angie.

"Clay? Travis?" Angie's anxious voice broke into the mounting tension between the two men.

Looking over Clay's shoulder, Travis saw her hurrying toward them as if her intervention might be needed at any minute. Which wasn't all that far from the truth, he admitted as she reached them.

"I wasn't expecting you, Clay." She moved past her brother to stand next to Travis.

"I was in the neighborhood and thought I'd stop and say hello. You were already in bed when I got home last night."

"Yes." She didn't bother to specify which bed she'd been in and Travis wasn't about to clarify the point.

There was an awkward silence and Travis saw Clay's eyes go from his sister's face to where her hand rested against Travis's hip, an intimacy Travis doubted she was even aware of. The same could not be said for her brother.

"Can I talk to you, Angie?"

"Not if you're just going to tell me to stay away from Travis again," she said bluntly.

From the angry flush that came up in Clay's cheeks, it was obvious that that was exactly what he'd had in mind. The look he shot Travis said that he knew exactly where to place the blame for Angie's sudden truculence.

"Angie . . ."

"No. I'm tired of these veiled warnings, Clay. If you've got something to say, then say it. But stop acting like an overprotective, Victorian big brother."

"Fine," he snapped, stung. "Just don't come crying to me when you find out I was right."

"I won't."

Stubbornness was obviously a family trait, Travis thought. The last thing he wanted was for Angie and Clay to back themselves into opposite corners, with him squarely in the middle. He'd already done enough damage. He didn't want to cause further tension between the two of them. Whether she knew it or not, Angie was going to need her brother's support sooner or later.

"Look, why don't you two talk this out," he said uncomfortably. "I'm really not worth all this trouble."

As an attempt to lighten the tension with a little humor, it failed abysmally. Angie's fingers hooked into the top of his belt, anchoring him in place. The look Clay shot him held no gratitude, only a bitter anger.

"I don't want to talk about it," Angie said, directing the words at her furious brother.

"You got it." Casting a fulminating look at Travis, he spun on his heel and stalked across the narrow parking lot to where his car was parked.

Neither Angie nor Travis said a word until the red T-Bird had roared out of the parking lot. It was left to Angie to break the silence.

"Honestly, from the way he treats me, you'd think I was five years old."

"He's worried about you."

"He's overbearing and obnoxious," she said, her voice still laced with annoyance.

"That, too, but he's still worried about you."

"Well, he shouldn't be. I'm a big girl now." She turned to face him. "And I'm perfectly capable of making up my own mind. Now, let's talk about something besides my overbearing brother.''

''Like what?''

''Like, have you missed me?'' She grinned up at him, her eyes sparkling.

''Some,'' he admitted, frowning as if grudging the admission.

''How much?'' She was wheedling shamelessly for compliments and Travis found himself wanting to grab her up in his arms and kiss her senseless.

''Enough that I've been wondering if I should ravish you in the bushes,'' he admitted, raising his eyebrows lasciviously.

''Ordinarily I'd be more than happy to take you up on that offer but those bushes have some very nasty thorns.''

''What are thorns when passion burns strong?'' he questioned dramatically.

''They're painful. That's what they are.'' Her pained expression drew a laugh from him.

''You know, I've always wondered what you'd look like in a uniform,'' he commented, studying the plain white dress she wore with a pair of thick-soled white shoes.

''It's hardly the peak of fashion.''

''It makes you look very efficient. Very nursely.''

Travis found his fingers searching for the clip that pulled her hair back from her face.

"Nursely? I don't think that's a word." Angie tilted her head to allow him to pull the clip loose. Her hair tumbled over his fingers.

"It is now," he murmured, continuing the conversation, though neither of them was paying much attention to it. "You have the most beautiful hair."

"Thank you. I like yours, too." She lifted one hand to ruffle her fingers through his dark blond hair.

Unable to resist temptation another moment, Travis bent to taste the softness of her mouth. It was a slow, thorough kiss that seemed to brand her as his. Angie felt her knees weaken as her hands came up to cling to his shoulders. Travis's arms tightened around her, molding her body to his, letting her feel his arousal, showing her how much he wanted her.

When he lifted his head, she drew a deep, shaken breath. It took a real effort to force her lashes up. Travis was looking down at her with the same puzzled expression she'd seen before, as if he wasn't quite sure she belonged in his arms.

But *she* was sure and she could be patient until he figured it out.

"I have to go. Janine's assisting the doctor and there's only so much she can do."

"Okay." Travis let his hands slide from her with obvious reluctance. "What time do you get off?"

"Six." Angie took her hair clip from him.

"Do you have plans for tonight?" There was a touch of hesitancy in the question as if he wasn't sure he wanted to ask it.

"Well, I had planned to wash my hair but I'm open to a better offer." The look she gave him was pure invitation and he wasn't proof against it.

"I'm a lousy cook but I do the best take-out Chinese you've ever seen," he said.

"I like moo shoo pork and I don't like those nasty little red peppers that set fire to your mouth," she said promptly. "Shall I bring anything?"

"Just yourself." As if unable to resist the urge, his hands caught her waist, pulling her close for a kiss that threatened to dissolve every bone in her body. When he released her, Angie had to cling to his shoulder until her knees were capable of supporting her again.

"Never mind the hot peppers," she murmured. "Another kiss like that and I'm likely to go up in smoke."

Travis returned her smile with a brooding look. "I don't want to hurt you, Angel," he said slowly.

"Oh, not you, too." Exasperated, she pushed out of his arms. "It's bad enough that Clay acts like I'm a helpless child. Don't you start it, too."

"I don't think you're a child." Travis shoved his hands into his pockets and continued to look at her broodingly. "I just want to be sure you're not going into this with your eyes shut."

"It's a little late to worry about that, don't you think? After last night?" There was more than a trace of irritation in her question.

He flushed but continued doggedly. "Maybe but I don't want you to mistake what's between us."

"And just what *is* between us, Travis?"

Neither of them was aware that they were standing in a parking lot in broad daylight. The traffic that moved on the busy streets, the heat that radiated off of pavement and walls—all were forgotten.

"What is between us?" she asked again, trying not to let him see how much his answer mattered.

"I...want you. So much I can hardly keep my hands off you," he admitted, his mouth twisting ruefully.

"And I want you," she said. "Is that all that's between us, then? Sexual attraction?"

His eyes searched hers, his a clouded green and full of secrets, hers shining blue and demanding honesty. For a moment, she thought he was going to open up to her, to let her inside the walls he used to keep the world at bay, but then he looked away, shoving his hands into his pockets and half shrugging.

"Sex can be a pretty powerful draw," he said, at last, almost as if he were talking to himself. "Especially when it seems new and fresh."

Angie felt a surge of crisp anger. So, not only was he not going to admit that he felt anything for her, but he was going to dismiss her feelings as nothing more than sexual need. If she hadn't been so sure that he *did* care, she might have been hurt. Instead, she felt a good, healthy anger.

"Well, sex is better than nothing," she said, shrugging lightly. She felt real satisfaction when Travis's eyes jerked to her face in shock. She pretended not to notice, glancing instead at her watch. "I've got to get going."

She braced her hands on his shoulders and raised on her toes to press her mouth to his. She felt his shock as her tongue came out to trace his lower lip. His hands caught her waist, bracing her automatically as she pressed closer, her mouth opening on his.

Angie intended the kiss to punish him for dismissing their relationship as purely sexual. She wanted to leave him with a vivid reminder that the sexual pull went both ways. She wasn't the only one caught in it.

Travis groaned softly as she slid her hands into his hair and arched against him, letting him feel every soft inch of her. The blood was pounding in his body, making it difficult to remember that they were standing in plain view of anyone who happened to walk by.

His hands started to slid around her back, to draw her even closer. But she was suddenly ending the kiss and slipping away from him.

"Got to go," she said, her casual tone only slightly marred by breathlessness. "I'll see you tonight."

She darted away with a quick wave of her hand, refusing to look back. If he thought he was the only one who could play stupid games, he had another think coming.

Chapter Ten

Travis hadn't been sure what to expect from Angie. Her mood had seemed odd when they parted. There'd been a sharpness in her he'd never seen before, an edge that he hadn't expected.

But none of that was evident when she arrived on his doorstep a little after seven. Though darkness was approaching, the heat lingered and she'd changed from her uniform into a sundress with a bright floral print that skimmed her body, hinting at more than it revealed.

There was no sign of her earlier mood as they ate Chinese food and argued over the relative merits of everything from Woody Allen movies to football scholarships. Travis found himself forgetting all the reasons their involvement was doomed to failure and simply enjoyed himself.

Though he wanted to believe otherwise, there was a great deal more between them than just physical desire. Powerful as that was, it wasn't all that drew him to her. He'd never known a woman who could make him laugh as easily as Angie did, who could argue passionately and yet never let the argument become personal.

He *liked* her, dammit. And if there was more to it than that, he'd be a fool to admit it, even to himself. Especially to himself.

He was surprised to realize that it was after ten when the conversation started to lag. They had moved from the kitchen to the living room, where the fan served to at least stir the warm air, giving the illusion of cooler temperatures.

Angie was curled in the big leather chair, her legs drawn up under her skirt and Travis had the fanciful thought that she looked like a multicolored flower, her skirt forming the petals that draped gracefully across the worn black leather.

Rather than trust the sofa, which was more bare springs than cushion, Travis had chosen to sit on the floor and lean back against it, stretching his legs out along the floor. The lamp cast a single circle of light in the dim room, as soft as candlelight.

It was a comfortable quiet, the sort that happens between two people who are past the stage of needing to fill every silence that falls between them. Travis leaned his head back against the sofa, and allowed his gaze to settle on Angie.

She was curled into the chair like a cat on a favorite cushion, her body relaxed against the leather, her eyes half closed as if she might fall asleep. His gaze drifted over her face, tracing the delicate line of her brows, the gentle curve of her mouth, the stubborn strength of her jaw.

From there it was a short trip to the soft length of her throat. The V-neck of her dress left her collarbone bare and he allowed his eyes to linger on the pulse that beat in the hollow of her throat. Since her shoulders were bare, it didn't seem likely that she was wearing a bra and he couldn't prevent his gaze from moving speculatively to the fullness of her breasts beneath the thin fabric of the dress.

Aware that he was growing uncomfortably aroused, he forced his eyes away from her, focusing instead on a hairline crack that ran down the wall near the door. *Probably caused by an earthquake,* he thought, trying to convince himself that he gave a damn.

"You know, I'm really glad we had that little talk today."

Travis started, his eyes jerking back to her.

"Little talk?" he questioned, momentarily at a loss.

"Yes. The one where you explained that what we have is a strong sexual attraction and nothing more."

"I didn't say that exactly." He watched warily as she uncurled her legs and rose. He'd almost managed to forget about that talk.

"Close enough." Angie didn't seem at all upset by the memory. "It made me think."

"It did?" He wasn't at all sure he was going to like the direction in which this conversation was going.

"Yes." She lifted her arms over her head, arching her back in a stretch. Travis's eyes dropped to the proud thrust of her breasts and he felt a wave of hunger.

Angie slanted him an unreadable look from under her lashes and reached behind her back. The unmistakable hiss of a zipper being lowered made Travis's mouth go dry.

"Yes, I thought about it quite a bit this afternoon." The dress loosened around her but didn't fall.

"You did?" He was no longer at all sure what they were discussing.

"I decided that, if sex is all we have going for us, we might as well make the most of it." She loosened the tie at the back of her neck and the dress slid down her body, landing in a bright splash of color on the floor.

And Travis forgot how to breathe.

Where on earth had she found a garment like that? Did she realize that something like that could give a man a heart attack? He wasn't even conscious of standing up.

Angie watched him from under her lashes, well satisfied with the results she'd achieved. He looked as if he'd been hit in the head with a baseball bat. She'd been a little uncertain when she dragged the black silk teddy from the back of her lingerie drawer. It had been a gift from her friend Leigh two birthdays ago and she'd never had a reason to wear it. Now she was glad she'd saved it.

She'd heard it said that sex was not enough to base a relationship on and she didn't doubt the truth of that. On the other hand, she had a heart-deep belief that Travis's feelings for her ran a lot deeper than he was willing to admit. Until the day came that he could face that, she wasn't above using sex to sharpen his interest.

If Travis could have read her thoughts he would have assured her that she'd succeeded in sharpening his interest. In fact, it was so sharp at the moment that if a Sherman tank had thundered through the wall, he would barely have noticed the intrusion.

He couldn't take his eyes off the way the strapless black silk cupped her breasts. If she drew a deep breath, she was surely going to spill out. He found himself praying for her to feel breathless.

He didn't remember moving but he was suddenly standing in front of her, his hands settling on her slender waist, drawing her closer. His blood pounded in his veins but he caught the flicker of uncertainty in her eyes as she lifted her hands to his shoulders. It reminded him of just how limited her experience was.

"From innocent to seductress in twenty-four hours," he said huskily. "Quite a transition."

"I aim to please," she told him.

"If you pleased me anymore, you just might kill me." His laugh held a note of real pain. "You shouldn't spring something like that on a man."

"I'll keep that in mind in the future."

Her words brought a quick frown. "In the future." Just what was that supposed to mean? Was she going to let someone else see her in this scrap of silk nothing. The thought had his hands tightening around her waist as he dragged her closer.

"You'd better never let anyone see you in that thing but me," he whispered against her mouth. His kiss was pure masculine possessiveness staking a claim.

Angie surrendered without protest. For now she'd accept possessiveness as a step in the right direction. Given time, possessiveness could grow into something deeper and more lasting. Something like love.

Passion flared hot and fast between them, burning away everything but need and a soul-deep hunger. If Travis's fingers were impatient with the thin silk that kept him from her skin, Angie's fingers trembled in their eagerness to rid him of the layers of cloth that separated them.

Travis barely retained enough self-control to get them into the bedroom. The springs creaked a protest as they fell onto the bed. Travis twisted so that Angie landed on top of him. Winding his hands in her hair, he dragged her mouth down to his. She tasted faintly of the beer she'd had after dinner. She felt like heaven.

Heat shot through him as she shifted, straddling his thighs. His hands left her hair to grasp her hips, lifting her, positioning and sliding into the welcome sheath of her all in one move. She accepted this new position without hesitation, her calves pressing against his thighs as she sat upright, taking him deeper.

He took hold of her hips, guiding her, helping her find a rhythm. But it wasn't long before the soft ripeness of her breasts became a temptation too great to resist. He watched her, wishing there was more light so that he could see the flush that rose from her breasts to her throat when she neared completion.

Angie felt herself trembling on the brink, a heartbeat away from the peak she knew lay just out of sight. Her whole being tensed with the need to reach that goal. It was so close, so very, very close.

And then Travis's fingers were touching her where their bodies joined together, finding the very heart of her need and she was tumbling headlong into a whirlpool of pure sensation. She heard Travis groan low in his throat and his hands were suddenly gripping her hips as he arched into her.

As the sensations ebbed, she collapsed onto his chest, her breathing ragged, her whole body limp and sated. Travis's hand came up to comb through her hair and she felt a purely feminine satisfaction when she realized that his fingers were not quite steady.

She didn't know how long they lay there, still linked physically and mentally. Travis's fingers continued to move through her hair, a soft rhythmic motion that made Angie feel like a particularly well-fed cat.

"Angel?" His voice was a husky rumble under her ear. She lifted her head to look into his face.

"What?"

"It's not just sex between us." The husky admission flowed over her like a warm summer's breeze.

"I know." She didn't press for more. It was enough for now that he'd admitted that much.

ANGIE DIDN'T KNOW what time it was when the sound of a phone ringing woke her. While she was still registering the sound, Travis was out of bed and on his way into the living room. The phone cut off in midring and then she heard the low murmur of his voice. The tone didn't sound urgent, though she couldn't distinguish what he was saying. It seemed as if she was still trying to clear the sleep from her eyes when he was sliding back between the sheets.

"Something wrong?" she asked as he drew her against him.

"No. Just a business call."

"At two in the morning?" She'd managed to focus on the clock next to the bed.

"It's not two in the morning all over the world," he said by way of explanation. "Go back to sleep."

Angie knew she hadn't heard the whole story but she also doubted that further questions would elicit anything but more evasions. Just what part of the world was Travis getting calls from? And what kind of work did he do that made calls in the middle of the night necessary?

Frowning slightly, she allowed her head to settle on his shoulder, throwing one arm across his chest. One of these days, she was going to get answers to all the questions she had about him. But not tonight.

Travis listened to her quiet breathing as she slid back to sleep. Things were moving faster than he'd expected. Shearson was back from Tahiti and he wanted a meeting. It was exactly what he'd been angling toward for weeks but he couldn't help but think that the timing stank.

Just a few more days, he thought. He'd wanted just a few more days with Angie before life intruded, but tonight was all he was sure of having. In the morning, he'd tell her that he couldn't see her for a while. He turned his face into her hair, savoring the soft scent that was hers alone.

God, Clay had been right. He had no business letting things go this far. He'd allowed his hunger for her warmth to cloud his judgment. He was only now facing just how difficult it was going to be to avoid hurting her badly.

How was he supposed to make her understand?

ANGIE PULLED HER CAR into the driveway and shut the engine off but she didn't immediately get out. Instead, she leaned her forearms on the steering wheel and stared out the windshield. The sun was barely up and traces of mist lingered under the branches of the big sycamore that all but filled the backyard. By ten, the mist would be gone as the summer sun consolidated its hold on Southern California.

Angie wasn't particularly interested in the weather at the moment. Her thoughts were on the man she'd just left, the man she'd managed to fall in love with. They'd just spent a most satisfactory night together and she'd awakened to find him kissing his way up the length of her spine, an action that had led to long and eminently pleasurable lovemaking.

And yet while they were dressing he'd told her that he couldn't see her tonight. As if she'd asked! Angie frowned and drummed her fingers against the steering wheel. He'd said he had business to attend to but, as usual, he hadn't bothered to specify just what that business was. Damn, the man was frustrating.

Why couldn't she have fallen in love with an accountant? Or a doctor? Why couldn't she have fallen in love with a man whose past wasn't a state secret and who didn't have such an aversion to talking about his present?

Because she'd fallen in love with Travis. The obvious answer didn't make her feel any better. She got out of the car and strode toward the house, her heels clicking on the pavement. Mysterious phone calls before dawn and then an announcement that he wouldn't be able to see her tonight. He'd said he wasn't wanted by the police and Clay had admitted that he wasn't a criminal. Then what was he?

She pulled open the kitchen door and stepped inside before realizing the room was already occupied. Clay stood next to the coffeemaker and from the way he turned to look at her, he had heard her coming.

Their eyes met for a moment and then Clay's dropped to skim over her dress and heels. It was obvious she'd been out all night. *And none of his business,* Angie reminded herself, lifting her chin as his gaze returned to her face.

"Good morning." She spoke first, deciding to treat the situation as if there was nothing unusual about it.

"Good morning." Clay hesitated but followed her lead.

Unfortunately Angie had run out of conversational gambits. They looked at each other across a gulf—a gulf neither was quite ready to bridge. After a moment, Clay turned away, rinsing his cup in the sink before setting it in the dishwasher.

"Well, I've got to get going if I'm going to get my run in before work." His voice was too hearty and his eyes avoided her as he turned from the sink.

"Yes." She wasn't sure what she was agreeing to but it seemed as if she should say something and that was all that occurred to her.

He glanced at her again and hesitated.

"Look, I know you don't want to hear it but I can't just watch you walk into this with your eyes closed."

"My eyes are wide open, Clay." But her tone held no anger. He looked so worried. "I'm not a fool."

"I know you're not." His fingers toyed restlessly with his watchband. "But you don't have all the facts. You don't know what Travis really is."

"I know he's the man I love," she said flatly. The words sounded surprisingly natural when spoken aloud. She saw their impact on her brother. He winced, his eyes closing for a moment. When they opened again, there was something approaching despair in their depths.

"Angie, there are things about Morgan that you don't know."

"I'm sure there's a lot I don't know," she agreed readily. "But I'd rather find out from him."

"But—"

"No, Clay. Please." She stretched one hand out, her expression pleading. "Unless you've got something concrete to tell me, I don't want to hear anymore. I don't want to hear what he might have been involved in when you were in high school. I don't want to hear what you suspect him of now. If you've got proof, tell me. Otherwise, leave it alone.''

Clay stared at her, frustration tying his gut in knots. He was torn between the need to protect her and his inability to reveal privileged information. There was really only one decision possible.

''Okay,'' he said tiredly. ''I'll keep my mouth shut about Morgan and let you do as you see fit.''

''Thank you.''

''But I'm still your big brother. And if you need me, I'm still here for you, just like always.''

''Just like always,'' Angie agreed softly.

He lifted one hand in farewell and walked out the door. Angie stood in the brightly lit kitchen, feeling more lonely than she'd ever felt in her life. From the time she was small, Clay had always been there for her. They'd never gone through a stage where they weren't friends, the way most brothers and sisters did.

He'd never minded her tagging along when he went fishing.It had been Clay who taught her to ride a bike. Clay who comforted her when their mother abandoned the family. When their father died, it was Clay who insisted that Angie stay with him, rather than being farmed out to more ''suitable'' care until her eighteenth birthday.

''Damn!'' She rubbed her fingers over her cheeks, unsurprised to find them damp. Her brother had always been one of her best friends. Why, all of a sudden, had he turned into something out of a Victorian novel?

Well, it would take time but he'd come around. Sooner or later he'd understand that she had to live her own life and make her own mistakes. She refused to believe that loving Travis was a mistake.

Her steps were slow as she climbed the stairs to her room. Yesterday morning, she'd practically floated up these stairs, sure that everything was going to turn out just as it should. But Clay's attitude and the secrecy with which Travis surrounded himself had taken their toll on that optimism.

"I'm just tired," she said aloud, her voice echoing in the hallway as she paused outside her bedroom door. Tired and just a little uncertain. What had happened to her life lately? Everything had changed so quickly. She rubbed a tired hand over her face. A couple of hours sleep would help to banish her doubts, she told herself briskly, pushing open the door.

As it turned out, she didn't have time to take a nap. Angie had no sooner stepped out of the shower than the phone range. The clinic was short on staff. Could Angie possibly come in early? She would have agreed to go in, even if she'd had other plans, but going to work just suited her mood this morning. The last thing she wanted was to have time to brood.

It was a busy day, for which Angie was grateful. She felt guilty about her gratitude. After all, a busy day in the clinic was hardly good news for the people coming in for help. But as long as she was occupied, she didn't have time to worry about the rift between her and Clay. Or to worry about just what Travis's "business" might be. Or to wonder when he'd call her. *If* he called.

Since she'd never been in love before, she'd never realized just how vulnerable the emotion would make her feel. She was *sure* Travis cared for her—until she thought about it a little too long. And then she was equally sure that he only desired her.

Angie murmured soothingly to a crying baby who was strenuously objecting to the treatment for a nasty scratch she'd received from a cat who didn't like having its neck squeezed. Even as Angie tended to the child, her hands sure and steady, part of her mind was occupied with the age-old question: Did he love her or didn't he?

She handed the crying infant to her mother, reassuring her that no permanent damage had been done. The woman was nearly in tears as she thanked Angie. Angie saw them on their way and then went to wash up before greeting the next patient.

She was a good nurse, she thought, glaring at the bottle of antiseptic soap as if daring it to deny that fact. She'd worked hard to get her training and she'd graduated among the top ten in her class. She was a strong, modern woman, not some fainting flower.

She'd watched her friend Leigh fall in and out of love half a dozen times since they were teenagers. And she'd never understood how Leigh could let her emotions get so completely out of control every time. Surely, *she'd* never be that way, if and when she fell in love.

And here she was, in love and a quivering mass of uncertainty and insecurity. Her mouth twisted in wry humor as she dried her hands. Maybe this was her comeuppance for being so smug and superior when Leigh was in the throes of each new love affair.

"Angie, the patient in two wants a tetanus shot."

Angie turned a quick smile on Hugh Johnson as the doctor stopped to wash his hands.

"No patient *wants* a tetanus shot, Hugh. Am I going to have to sit on this one?"

"It's Mrs. Ludovich," he told her as he soaped his hands. "She cut herself and she's convinced lockjaw is only a heartbeat away."

"Lockjaw? Mrs. Ludovich?" Angie widened her eyes, picturing the elderly woman who was known for her ability to talk for half an hour without pausing for air. "Lockjaw wouldn't have a chance with her," she said.

"Probably not." Hugh Johnson's serious features creased in a rare smile. "To tell the truth, I thought of prescribing twenty-four hours of silence just to see if she could stick to it.''

"Not a chance." Laughing, Angie left him and went to give Mrs. Ludovich her shot.

BY SEVEN O'CLOCK in the evening, she'd put in almost twelve hours, most of it on her feet. She'd given shots, patched minor injuries, listened sympathetically when that seemed the best medicine she could offer. Her feet hurt, her back ached and she wanted nothing so much as a hot shower and a bed. But the hours of work had served to distract her. It wasn't possible to worry about Clay and Travis and simultaneously convince a fractious toddler that a shot was really a good thing.

The clinic closed at seven-thirty, leaving the emergency room of the local hospital to pick up the burden after that. At seven-twenty, Angie was cleaning one of the examining rooms and trying to decide whether or not to stop on the way home to pick up a salad for dinner.

At seven-twenty-five, the front door flew open and the quiet was shattered by the sound of shouted demands for help, mixed with moans of pain and hysterical sobbing.

Angie flew out of the examining room, entering the waiting room hard on Hugh Johnson's heels. The room seemed full of people at first. It took several minutes for Angie to sort them out. There were two youths in their early twenties, their decorated vests identifying them as members of a local gang. Between them they held up a boy who looked no more than thirteen. Angie barely noticed the older woman behind the three, the source of the sobbing.

"What happened?" Hugh snapped out the question, even as he was reaching for the boy.

"It was an accident," one of the youths muttered, exchanging a look with his friend.

"An accident!" That was the older woman, whom Angie had already pegged as the wounded boy's mother. "They've killed him with their stupid wars. My baby, who never hurt anyone. I told you what would happen if you joined that gang. Now look at your brother!"

"Gunshot wounds," Hugh told Angie, ignoring the woman's continued recriminations. "He's lost a lot of blood."

"Can we get him to General?" The hospital was better equipped to handle a gunshot wound, but Hugh was already shaking his head.

"We've got to try to stop the bleeding, at least. We'll put him in number one. Janine, call General. Tell them what we've got."

"Yes, Doctor." Janine turned to the phone even as Hugh directed the two youths to help him get the boy into the examining room he'd indicated.

"Is he going to be all right?" That was the boy's brother as Angie urged them from the room. Looking at his white face and frightened eyes, she wanted to offer him some reassurance but there wasn't anything she could say.

"Dr. Johnson is an excellent doctor," she said. "We'll do the best we can." She pushed them from the room and turned back to where Hugh was cutting open the boy's shirt to get a better look at the wounds.

One of the most difficult lessons for any medical professional to learn is that doing their best sometimes just isn't enough. No matter how much skill and concern were brought to bear, they couldn't win every battle.

Angie and Hugh were fighting a losing battle from the beginning and they knew it. One look at the wounds and the amount of blood the boy had already lost and they both knew what his chances were. But they didn't hesitate.

They immediately went to work, attempting to stop the seemingly inexhaustible flow of blood. They'd worked together for over a year now and Angie was able to anticipate his needs before he expressed them. Moving as if they'd been choreographed, they fought to save the boy's life.

Though Angie had never heard Hugh say so much as "damn," she wasn't shocked by the steady stream of curses that left him when it became obvious that this was one battle they weren't going to win.

By the time paramedics arrived, there was nothing they could do. There'd been nothing they could have done from the start. Angie stood in one corner of the examining room, watching as they transferred the body to a stretcher and pulled the sheet up over the young face. Her hands hung limp at her sides. She couldn't think of a better place to put them.

A glance at the clock told her that barely twenty minutes had passed since she'd been thinking about what to do for dinner. Twenty minutes. It seemed like hours. Moving as if she were an old woman, she began cleaning the examining room, her movements automatic.

"Leave it." That was Hugh, coming back into the room. His thin body radiated defeat. "I'll clean up."

"I don't mind." Angie methodically gathered the bloodstained instruments together.

"Leave it," he said again. "Go home. You've been here all day."

"So have you," she pointed out.

"Yeah." He stared around the small room for a moment and then went to rub his fingers over his eyes. He stopped, the move uncompleted as he stared at the blood on his hands. "Jesus, some days I hate this job."

In the end, they cleaned up together, finding some solace in the mundane tasks. When it was done, they left the clinic, parting company without a word. There just didn't seem to be anything to say.

Angie started her car and pulled out of the parking lot but, instead of turning left toward home, she found herself turning right. The only thing she could think of was that she had to see Travis. She wanted to feel his arms around her and have him tell her that everything was going to be all right.

It no longer mattered that she didn't know how he felt about her. She didn't care what his mysterious business was. She didn't care about anything but seeing him.

Chapter Eleven

Travis's thoughts were on the upcoming meeting with Shearson's minions. He'd spent months working toward it and he hadn't expected this break so soon. It was everything he'd worked for and it was dropping into his lap like a ripe plum.

The meeting was set for ten o'clock at a local bar. Shearson wasn't particularly concerned about whether the police found out that he was thinking of taking on a new middleman. They'd find out sooner or later anyway. The bar was public and it was noisy, and if Shearson's men were known to the police, the police were also known to them and they'd be very visible.

When someone knocked on the door, Travis's hand jerked toward the gun he wore tucked into the back of his belt. *Nervous reflex*, he told himself but he didn't release the gun. Who the hell was banging on the door now?

"Travis?" He glanced at the clock and cursed softly. He'd told Angie he couldn't see her tonight. What was she doing here?

"Travis?" She knocked again, her voice sounding thin and uncertain in a way he'd never heard before.

"Damn." He moved to the door and pulled it open, his expression less than welcoming.

But he forgot all about his irritation and the upcoming meeting when he saw her. Her hair fell in untidy straggles from where it was caught on top of her head. Her face was pale and drawn with dark hollows under her eyes. But what caught his eyes and caused his mouth to go dry with fear were the bloodstains that streaked garishly across the formerly pristine fabric of her uniform.

"My God, Angie. What happened?" He reached out and caught her in his arms, pulling her into the living room and kicking the door shut behind them.

"Oh, Travis. There was nothing we could do." The words ended on a shallow sob. Her arms came up to circle his neck and she leaned into him like a tired child.

Relieved that none of the blood was hers, Travis put his arms around Angie and drew her closer. She shuddered and began to cry softly, as if all she'd needed was his touch to release the dammed-up tears.

It took her some time to get her tears under control. By then, from her assorted muffled explanations,

Travis had managed to get a fairly clear picture of what had happened to upset her so much.

Angie had no clear memory of him settling in the big leather chair and then pulling her onto his lap. She also didn't remember his pulling the pins from her hair but he must have because he was now combing his fingers through it in a wonderfully soothing rhythm.

"He was so young, Travis," she whispered, her voice husky from crying.

"Try not to think about it."

"He'd lost so much blood. There just wasn't anything we could do."

"You did the best you could. It's not your fault he didn't make it."

"I know." She sighed and let her head fall against his shoulder. "It just seems like there *should* have been something we could have done. I felt so helpless. So useless."

Travis put his fingers under her chin and raised her face to his. "You did everything you could, Angie. You're not God."

"I know." She knew he was right but knowing didn't take away the feeling that she'd failed the boy.

Travis read the doubt in her eyes and knew she was a long way from accepting that there was nothing she could have done to save the boy. He cupped her face in his hands, kissing the dampness from her cheeks.

He wanted to take her hurt away, make it his own. He wanted to hold her close and make sure that nothing could ever hurt her again.

"I couldn't think of where else to come," she admitted tiredly. "I forgot that you'd said you had things to do tonight."

"That's okay." He settled her back against his shoulder and glanced at his watch. Much as he longed to let the meeting go hang, there was too much riding on it. "I have to go out in a little while," he told her.

"I should go." But she wasn't sure she had the strength to get up, let alone the energy to drive home.

"No." His arm tightened around her. "I won't be gone long. You can wait here and I'll take you home later, if you want."

"All right." Vaguely she thought that she shouldn't agree so easily. Hadn't she spent most of the day debating his feelings for her? But that no longer seemed important. When she'd been in pain, she'd turned to him instinctively and he was there for her. Maybe that was enough for now.

"Morgan." The knock on the door shattered the peaceful atmosphere but it was the sound of his name that had an electric effect on Travis. With a low oath, he scooped her up on his lap and stood up, setting her on her feet in one smooth move. He stood beside her, every muscle taut, his eyes on the door. When she started to ask what was wrong, he lifted his hand to his mouth, silencing her.

He grabbed hold of her wrist and looked around the bare room as if seeking a place to hide her. His visitor knocked again, a little louder this time.

"Come on, Morgan. Open up." The tone was so demanding that Angie's first thought was that it was the police but something in the taut lines around Travis's eyes told her that that wasn't the case. Unless he really *was* wanted by the police.

He pulled her toward the bedroom and thrust her through the door. "Stay in here and don't say a word. No matter what you hear or think you hear, don't come out. Do you understand?"

"I understand. But what's going on?"

A third round of knocking, even more impatient than the last had him glancing over his shoulder, her question forgotten.

"If there's trouble, go out the bedroom window and run like hell. *Don't* come out. No matter what you hear. Do you understand me?"

"But what's—"

"Do you understand me?" His hands tightened on her shoulders, his eyes fierce and urgent.

"Yes." Angie felt fear uncurl in the pit of her stomach. What was going on here?

"Travis." But he was gone, drawing the door shut behind him, leaving Angie alone in the dark bedroom. Alone and scared to death.

TRAVIS FORCED his thoughts away from Angie as he moved to open the door. He couldn't afford to think of her now, couldn't afford to think of anything but the goal he'd worked so long and so hard to achieve. This visit wasn't part of the plan and he didn't particularly like surprises, not at this stage of the game. But Shearson *did* like surprises, especially when he was the one delivering them. He could only hope that this surprise was not going to be nasty.

He pulled open the door and scowled at the two men on the doorstep. One of them had unscrewed the bulb in the porch light so they stood in darkness, but enough light spilled out the door for Travis to identify them. Drasen and Sinclair. Not too fondly known as the Dragon and the Saint. Drasen for his size and fierce reputation, Sinclair for his habit of attending church faithfully every Sunday.

He'd known them both years ago. After he left, they became Shearson's right-hand men. They were quick and dangerous, giving no more thought to killing a man than most people did to blowing their nose. He wondered if he should be flattered that Shearson had sent both of them.

"What the hell are you doing here?" he demanded, taking the initiative.

"Could we discuss this inside?" Sinclair asked politely. "My companion is feeling a trifle exposed."

Travis hesitated a moment, as if considering kicking them off his porch, and then stepped back to allow them inside. "I thought we were going to meet at the Club," he said irritably, shutting the door behind his unwanted guests.

He should have been expecting this, he thought. Shearson was fond of springing surprises, frequently unpleasant ones. He believed that keeping his people off balance was good for them. Considering the success of his organization, Travis couldn't argue with the policy. He hoped that surprise was all Sinclair and Drasen had brought with them.

"We decided it was too public," Drasen said.

"I was just about to leave," Travis said, making his annoyance plain.

"And leave your guest?" Sinclair's eyes went to the bedroom door and then shifted back to Travis's face, cool and questioning.

Angie's car. Damn his stupidity. It was undoubtedly parked at the curb. And if they'd planned to show up here all along, they'd probably been watching when she arrived.

"She can wait." He shrugged to show how unimportant she was.

"A cop's sister," Sinclair commented, dashing the hope that they didn't know who she was. "A risky proposition, don't you think?"

"No." Travis met his eyes with an icy look. "Who's going to be suspicious of a guy who's dating a detective's sister?"

It was thin—it was very thin—but it was the best he could come up with spur-of-the-moment.

"Perhaps." Sinclair still looked doubtful but he was willing to let the subject go for now. "We've been told you can meet our requirements at a fair price," he continued, getting on to the reason for their meeting. "Our employer would like to see a sample of the merchandise. We have certain standards to maintain."

"I bet you do." Travis's grin was vulpine, his lean features hard in the dim light. Moving to the rickety sofa, he lifted one of the cushions and reached into a hole in the upholstery beneath. He came up with a small plastic bag and turned back to the two men.

"Not the best place of concealment," Sinclair commented.

"The cops have no reason to be interested in me." Travis lifted one shoulder to show his lack of concern. "Not yet, anyway."

Drasen took the bag from him and opened the upper corner. He licked his finger and touched the white powder it contained. Licking his finger, he frowned and then nodded. "It's pure." He resealed the bag carefully and weighed it in his hand. "There's more where this came from?"

"I can supply what you need." Travis saw the big man's eyes go to the sofa and he grinned again. "I don't keep it here, of course."

"Of course." That was Sinclair. "When can you make your first delivery?"

"I don't deal with flunkies," Travis said flatly. "If Shearson wants what I have, he can tell me himself."

It was a calculated risk. It could backfire on him. But he was suddenly impatient with all the games. He wanted this settled. He wanted to know where he stood.

Drasen stiffened, his broad features flushing with anger. Sinclair was made of cooler stuff. He merely raised one thin brow and looked almost amused. Sinclair would be the one to watch in a fight, Travis thought. He was ice cool and deadly.

"We're in a position to make you an offer, Mr. Morgan. We have all the authority."

"I deal with Shearson or I don't deal at all."

"Why?"

"I'm a cautious sort," Travis said coolly. "I figure if I'm dealing directly with the man in charge, there's less chance of a double-cross. I know him well enough to know he's not going to want to get caught in any nasty situations. If he wants what I have, he'll see me."

He could feel the adrenaline pumping through him, telling him he was on the right track. Playing along wasn't going to get him anywhere. Sheer arrogance just might.

His eyes locked with Sinclair's as the other man weighed his words and tried to decide whether he was serious. Whatever he saw must have convinced him because he lifted his narrow shoulders in a light shrug.

"We'll tell our employer what you've said. I doubt he'll agree to it."

"His choice." Travis shrugged his indifference. "I can always take my product elsewhere. He knows me well enough to know I can do it. You can take that sample to him. Tell him there's plenty more where that came from." Considering the street value of the cocaine in the bag Drasen held, it was an expensive gesture of good faith. But you didn't hook a shark without offering impressive bait.

"You seem very confident," Sinclair commented, showing a touch of curiosity.

"I know what I've got. And I know how much he wants it."

"Overconfidence can be a very dangerous thing."

"When you own a goose that lays golden eggs, there's no such thing as overconfidence."

"True." Sinclair nodded to Drasen who slipped the packet of cocaine into his inside jacket pocket. "*If* you own the only such goose," he warned. "We'll give our employer your message and get back to you."

"You do that."

Travis saw them out, feeling the adrenaline still pumping through his body. When they passed on his demand, Shearson might be annoyed but he'd also be interested. And he needed the coke. Despite Sinclair's cool facade, Travis could smell the hunger. Something had happened to their line of supply and they needed a new supplier. And they needed it now.

Grinning like a fool, he spun away from the door.

And met Angie's horrified gaze.

He'd been so focused on the battle of wits with Sinclair, he'd put her out of his mind completely. He'd concentrated completely on the task at hand, on the goal he'd been striving toward for so many months.

"You're dealing drugs."

The hushed accusation doused his euphoric mood instantly. His smile faded, replaced by an expressionless mask.

"You're dealing drugs," she said again, as if only by repeating the words could she make herself believe them. She came farther into the room, stopping a few feet away.

"Travis?" The plea in her voice went straight to his heart.

"What?" He forced himself to indifference.

"Aren't you going to say anything? There . . . there must be some explanation . . . ." She let the words trail off, obviously unable to think of such an explanation herself. "Maybe I misunderstood?" she suggested hopefully.

She was all but begging him to assure her that that was the case. Travis stared at her without saying a word. He wanted to go to her, hold her, tell her that it wasn't true. But he didn't move. Wasn't this just what he'd been looking for? A way to break off with her? A way to keep her away? Keep her safe.

But not like this, a voice inside him protested. She was looking at him as if she was seeing him for the first time—and not particularly liking what she saw.

Well, he never expected to win friends with what he was doing.

But not Angie. He didn't care what anyone else believed about him, but the look in Angie's eyes was like a knife in his chest.

"You didn't misunderstand," he said finally, when the silence had stretched to breaking point.

"Oh, God." The words were more prayer than curse. She'd been pale to begin with but the last traces of color drained away, leaving her ashen. "Oh, God."

She groped for something to lean on and set her hand on the back of the leather chair, the one they'd shared just a few minutes before, when she'd sat on his lap and let him soothe some of her pain away. But he couldn't soothe this pain away.

"How could you?" she asked at last, her voice hardly more than a whisper. "You know what drugs have done to the young people in this area. You've seen what happens to them. How could you?''

''I don't sell drugs to kids,'' he said automatically and then immediately regretted offering such a thin defense.

''Maybe not. But *they* do.''

Travis looked away from her, unable to face the bitter hurt in her face. What a mess. Why hadn't he listened to his common sense, not to mention her brother? He'd had no business getting involved with her. It had been doomed to disaster from the beginning.

''Aren't you going to say anything?''

''What do you want me to say?'' he asked wearily.

''I want you to tell me this is some kind of nightmare. I want you to tell me none of this is happening.''

''I wish I could.'' He thrust his fingers through his hair, feeling old and tired.

''How could you do this, Travis?'' Her voice broke on the question and Travis felt her pain as if it were his.

All he had to do was offer her an explanation. She'd believe anything he told her, at least for now. Later, she'd start to question, first herself and then him. And what could he say?

So he stayed silent.

When it became clear that he wasn't going to answer her question, Angie felt something shatter inside her. Her faith in him, in the future, in herself. How could she have thought she was in love with this man when it was obvious she didn't know him at all?

And the most terrible thing of all was that the love didn't die now that she knew what he was.

"I love you." The words were flat, without emotion. Angie saw Travis's head jerk up, his eyes startled. She pushed her hair back from her face, trying not to remember how he'd pulled the pins out and stroked his fingers through it, comforting her grief.

"Damn you!" Her voice broke as the pain stabbed in her chest. "Damn you, Travis!" Her fingers dug into the upholstery as she bent over the back of the chair, a shudder of agony racking her body.

"Angel . . ." He took a step toward her, half reaching out, as if to take her in his arms.

"Don't call me that!" Angie straightened instantly, her spine rigid, her eyes fierce. "And don't you dare touch me! Not ever again. Do you hear me?"

"I hear you." He faced her across the width of the big chair. Less than three feet separated them but it might as well have been three miles.

"I may love you but it doesn't matter," she told him.

Travis wanted to tell her that it mattered a great deal to him but the tangled web of lies and half-truths that surrounded them kept him silent.

"I can't accept what you're doing," she said flatly.

"I understand." He hardly knew what he was saying. He didn't understand anything, least of all his own reaction to her words.

"I have to go." Angie pulled her gaze away from his, looking around distractedly. "I have to go," she said again, more to herself than to him.

She moved toward the door, only to have Travis's words stop her.

"What are you going to do?"

"Do?" She turned to look at him, feeling her stomach twist in pain. "What do you mean?"

"Are you going to tell your brother about this?"

What did he expect her to say? Angie stared at him, trying to read his expression. But there was nothing there to read. They might have been talking about the weather, for all the concern she could read in his face.

How could he ask her such a thing? He'd put her in a miserable position. Either she ignored the worst kind of criminal behavior, or she did what she knew was right and helped send him to prison. And he wanted to know what choice she was going to make?

Travis regretted the question as soon as it was out. Damn his quick tongue! The torture in her eyes went through him as sharp as a knife.

"I don't know," she said, her voice thin and full of pain. "I don't know." She turned and left as if afraid he might say something more.

What could he have said? Travis stared at the closed door, feeling as if he'd been swept up in a whirlwind, given a thorough shaking and then set back down again.

The sound of Angie's car pulling away from the curb shook him out of his stupor. Moving slowly, he walked to the door and flipped the dead bolt shut. He leaned his forehead against the blank panel and closed his eyes.

What a night!

Dragging himself upright, Travis moved into the kitchen and got a beer out of the refrigerator. He twisted the top off the bottle but didn't lift it to his mouth. Instead, he stared at the refrigerator door, listening to the uneven whir of its motor and tried to sort out the night's events. What should he have done differently?

He couldn't have sent Angie away when she was in such pain. Even if he'd foreseen the arrival of Drasen and Sinclair, there wasn't much he could have done to prevent it. And once they were there and Angie was there, he supposed the rest had been inevitable.

Shaking his head, he lifted the beer and took a long swallow before moving back into the living room. He pushed the switch on the fan and it started sluggishly, stirring the warm air. Next time he rented a place in the summer, he was going to make sure the windows opened, he thought absently.

She'd said she loved him.

That was the thought he'd been trying to avoid since she left. The one thing that was impossible to forget. She loved him. Somewhere, deep inside, he felt a stirring that he recognized dimly. It was a warmth he'd never felt before.

She'd said she loved him. Even when she believed he was selling drugs, she'd still loved him. Hated him, too, of course, if he could judge by her expression. But who could blame her, believing what she did?

How many years had it been since he'd thought about things such as falling in love? How old had he been when he accepted that his parents would never love him quite as much as they loved each other and their wandering life-style?

He'd long ago come to terms with reality. He simply wasn't destined for the sort of home and hearth life that drew most men sooner or later. He didn't particularly mind. Domesticity seemed vastly overrated. He liked his work, enjoyed the company of women who were no more interested in settling down than he was. It was a perfectly good life-style.

And then he'd met Angie Brady.

He'd never before realized what a lethal combination big blue eyes and sunshine-colored hair could be. Suddenly he was thinking about picket fences and how nice it would be to share his life with someone. Someone who loved him. Someone he . . . loved.

Someone like Angie.

It was ironic that he was only able to admit that he loved her now that he'd lost her for good. Travis sank into the big leather chair and leaned his head back, closing his eyes. How had he managed to get his life so tangled up? He'd fallen in love and been too blind to know it, he thought.

Why hadn't he told her the truth? If not at the beginning, then tonight? Because, once he told her he loved her, he wasn't at all sure he'd be able to keep his distance from her, no matter what was at stake.

He shook his head, opening his eyes to stare blindly at the water-stained wallpaper opposite. He had to let it alone. There was no explanation he could offer, at least none that she would believe.

And she was better off out of it, out of his life. Her brother had been right from the beginning: He was not the kind of man she should know. He hadn't meant to hurt her but that's what he'd done.

She loved him.

And he'd lost her.

The bottle flew across the room, shattering against the wall, the contents staining the wallpaper. Travis closed his eyes, his fingers digging into the arms of the chair as he fought the urge to get up and put his fist through a wall.

For the first time in his life, he'd had something worth fighting for. And he'd just destroyed it.

Chapter Twelve

Angie stood in the shower and let the hot water pound over her. Her throat felt tight and her eyes ached but she could find no tears. She'd shed them all earlier, crying over the patient they hadn't been able to save. She didn't have any tears left for this second, more personal death. She set one arm against the tile and leaned her forehead on it, trying to absorb what had happened.

Travis was dealing drugs.

She couldn't make the words real, no matter how many times she repeated them to herself. There was a part of her that couldn't accept their truth. It didn't matter that she'd actually heard him arranging to meet with someone to discuss a drug deal. There had to be some other explanation.

Only he hadn't offered one.

He was selling drugs. She had to face it. Accept the reality of it, no matter how much it hurt.

Almost anything else she could have found a way to accept. But not this. This was one thing she could never accept, never condone. She'd seen the results of drug abuse firsthand. She knew what it did to the people who took drugs and what it did to their families. And she had nothing but contempt for the vultures who grew rich selling their poisons to kids too young and too foolish to know better.

And Travis was one of them.

With a moan, Angie turned her face into the hot spray of water, praying that it would wash away some of the pain. But it was going to take more than water to ease this pain. She doubted anything ever would.

She shut the water off but made no move to get out of the tub. Watching rivulets of water run down the shower door, she tried to think of where she should go from here. What was she going to do? Travis had asked the question. She hadn't had an answer then and she didn't seem to be any closer to one now.

Her movements sluggish, Angie slid open the shower door and reached for a towel. She dried herself, trying to concentrate on the simple task, trying to block out everything but the necessity of blotting every drop of water from her skin.

It was as she was reaching for her robe that she caught a glimpse of her reflection in the mirror. She stopped and stared at her image. The woman in the mirror was a little paler than usual perhaps. If you looked carefully, you might notice that her eyes seemed a little haunted, a little hollow. But there was no dramatic change outside to signal the turmoil inside.

Angie pulled her robe on slowly, wondering how she could look the same when she felt like a total stranger to herself. She wasn't the same woman she'd been a few short weeks ago. Her calm, safe existence had been shattered and she couldn't even begin to imagine how she was going to pick up the pieces.

She left the bathroom and went down the hall to her bedroom. Clay's car had been gone when she got home and there was no sign that he'd come back while she was showering. She was grateful for his absence. She didn't know if she could face him without blurting out the truth about Travis. And she didn't want to do that until she was sure it was the right thing to do.

Closing her bedroom door behind her, she waited for the peace she always felt there to enfold her. She'd grown from a child to a woman in this room. It knew all her secrets, all her dreams. It had been her haven through all the usual childish trials and tribulations.

But tonight it was just a room. She didn't feel any magical easing of her pain when she entered it. And she didn't find the answers she needed in the pictures on the walls or the row of childish stuffed toys that marched along a shelf near the ceiling.

The answers she needed were only going to be found in her heart. But how was she supposed to sort them out when all she could feel was pain?

Curling up in the wing chair that had been her fifteenth birthday present from her father, Angie drew her feet up onto the seat and wrapped her arms around them, laying her head on her knees and closing her eyes, wishing she could go back to that day.

She'd been so happy. So excited. The chair had made her feel like an adult and she'd made Clay move it to every possible position in her room before she'd finally settled on a place next to the window, where she could sit and watch the world go by and feel like a lady of the manor.

In retrospect, those days seemed idyllic. She'd had the usual teenage angst and there'd been times when she was convinced she was the most miserable girl on the face of the earth—or at least in the state of California. But they'd been good times, she thought now, even if she didn't believe it then.

No matter how hard she wished, she couldn't go back to being fifteen again. She was twenty-five and she'd just found out that the man she loved was selling drugs. And what made it even more terrible was that she still loved him.

Angie squeezed her eyes shut, feeling the sting of tears for the first time. How was it possible to love someone and hate what they were? What had happened to her that she could still love him, even knowing what he was? Why didn't finding out about the drugs erase her feelings for him?

Because she couldn't forget that this was the same man who'd come to her rescue when Billy Sikes and his gang were harassing her; the same man who'd slipped money to Mrs. Aggretti and then invented a job for her so she wouldn't feel like a charity case.

Knowing what he was didn't make her forget the way his eyes could smile even when his mouth remained serious. Or the way his mouth felt on hers. She couldn't forget the way he'd made love to her, treating her as if she were the most precious thing in the world to him. Her pleasure had come before his, he'd made sure of that.

The good memories didn't suddenly vanish. If they had, she wouldn't be torturing herself over what to do now. How was it possible that everything had fallen apart so quickly?

SITTING THERE, wrapped in pain, Angie lost track of the hours. She heard Clay come in, heard his footsteps going down the hall, hesitating outside her door. She bit her lip against the urge to call out to him. Her big brother had always been able to solve her problems for her, but this was one she had to decide on her own.

After a moment, he moved on and she heard his bedroom door close behind him. And then she put her head down on her knees and let the tears flow. Because she knew there really was no decision to make. There was only one choice, at least for her. Only one choice she could live with. And that one was unbearable.

ANGIE MUST HAVE DOZED off sometime near dawn because she woke when she heard the sound of Clay's bedroom door closing. She lifted her head, grimacing as her neck twinged in protest. For one blessed moment, she didn't remember why she'd fallen asleep in the chair. But memory came crashing in on her when she heard Clay running down the stairs.

She had to talk to him. And she had to talk to him now, this morning, before she found a way to talk herself out of it. She scrambled out of the chair, stumbling as her legs, cramped from her unusual choice of beds, threatened not to support her.

Clay was making coffee when she entered the kitchen. He was dressed for his morning run in shorts and T-shirt and the look he turned on her was not particularly welcoming.

''Good morning,'' he said coolly, before turning back to the coffeemaker.

Angie stared at his back, confused for a moment until she remembered their quarrel over Travis. She'd forgotten all about it. That seemed like years ago.

"Can I talk to you?" she asked, her voice husky with sleep and the tears she'd shed the night before.

"I don't have much time. Is it important?" He didn't turn to look at her as he spoke. Tears started to sting her eyes and were immediately suppressed. She'd cried enough.

"Travis is dealing drugs."

The bald statement sounded even harsher in the sunny kitchen than it had when she'd said it to herself.

"What!" Coffee scattered across the counter and onto the floor as Clay spun to face her, the measure still in his hand.

"I found out last night." She wrapped her arms around her waist and looked at the floor between them.

"How did you find out?" Clay had recovered from the initial shock. He set the measure down and punched the button to turn the coffeemaker on before turning back to her.

"I went to his house. He'd told me he was going to be busy but there was a boy brought into the clinic. He'd been shot. We couldn't save him." The words caught in her throat as she remembered how helpless they'd been.

"I heard about the shooting. I didn't know he'd been taken to the clinic." Clay crossed to her and put his arms around her. "I'm sorry, Angie. That must have been hell."

"It was rough." She slid her arms around his waist and let him hold her just as he had when she'd been six years old and her dog had been hit by a car. "He was so young, Clay."

"I know, half-pint." The old endearment made her want to break down and sob. But that wouldn't solve anything.

She drew in a deep breath and pulled away from him, her fingers tightening the belt of her robe, though it wasn't loose. It seemed to be getting harder to talk instead of easier. She let him lead her to one of the stools that sat next to the work island.

"So you went to see Morgan," he prompted gently.

"I went to see Travis," she confirmed. "I was so upset, I'd forgotten all about his saying he would be busy."

"What happened?"

"He held me and told me I'd done my best and I just had to accept that I wasn't God and couldn't save everyone." The memory stabbed at her. "He was so gentle," she whispered, more to herself than her brother.

"Then what?"

"Then, these two men showed up."

"Did you see them? Did they see you?" He sounded more like a cop than a brother and she responded automatically to his authoritative tone.

"No. Travis shoved me into the bedroom and told me not to come out, no matter what. He also said that if there was trouble I was to go out the window and run like hell," she said slowly, just now remembering his words, remembering the urgency in his face. He'd been worried about her safety, she thought. But there was no time to consider that because Clay was prodding her for the rest of the story.

"Did you hear what they were saying?"

"Some of it. They knew I was there," she said, remembering. "Maybe they saw my car. I don't know." She ran her fingers through her hair, wishing her brain didn't feel as if it were filled with lead.

"Travis seemed so upset that I listened at the door," she admitted. "I was worried about him." The irony of that struck her now, sending pain knifing through her. She had been worried about a drug dealer.

"What did they say? Did you get any names?"

"I don't think they gave their names but they mentioned someone named Shearson." She stopped as Clay's breath hissed between his teeth. His face was set and grim, what she'd always privately called his "cop face."

"What is it, Clay? Do you know who Shearson is?"

"Maybe." He got up, avoiding her questioning look as he went to pour coffee into two mugs. Angie didn't say anything more until he'd set a cup in front of her.

"Go on," he ordered shortly.

"They talked and it was obvious the two men worked for this Shearson and that Travis had something they wanted."

"Did they mention drugs?"

"Not specifically. But it was obvious what they were talking about. They asked if Travis had a sample and then a couple of minutes later one of them said 'It's pure.'"

She told him everything she remembered, including the way Travis had demanded a meeting with Shearson.

"That's about it, I guess. They said that they'd tell their boss what Travis wanted but they didn't think he'd agree to it. Travis didn't seem worried. He said Shearson knew him well enough to know he meant what he said. And then they left."

"Stupid," Clay muttered, as if to himself.

"What? What's stupid?" Angie was getting the distinct feeling that there were two conversations going on here and that she was only hearing one of them.

"Nothing. Did you confront Travis?"

"Yes. I suppose that was stupid. I mean, obviously, he's not the man I thought he was," she admitted painfully. "I suppose I should have pretended that I hadn't heard a thing."

"What did he say?"

"Nothing."

"Nothing?" Clay seemed surprised. "He didn't deny it or say he could explain?"

"He just said I hadn't misunderstood."

"Fool," Clay muttered.

Angie stiffened, feeling a spurt of anger. She hadn't expected a lot of sympathy from him but neither had she expected him to be so completely insensitive to her hurt.

"I know you told me to stay away from him," she said stiffly. "But I don't think 'I told you so' is going to do anyone any good at this point. And I don't particularly appreciate being called a fool, even if I was one."

"What?" Clay blinked and looked at her as if only just realizing she was there.

"I said, I don't like being called a fool," she snapped, hurt by his apparent lack of interest.

"I wasn't talking about you, half-pint. I was talking about Morgan."

"Oh." She was surprised that he hadn't come up with a stronger word to describe Travis. "Fool" seemed a mild epithet for someone who was selling drugs.

They were silent for a little while. Angie wrapped her hands around her cup, wishing the warmth of the coffee could penetrate deep enough to thaw the ice that had formed around her heart.

She'd done the right thing, she told herself. She'd done the only thing she could do. But that didn't stop her from feeling as if she'd betrayed Travis.

"What are you going to do?" she asked at last, unconsciously echoing Travis's question to her the night before.

"About Travis, you mean?"

"Yes." She ground her teeth together against the urge to beg him to let Travis go. To make him leave town but not to arrest him.

"You really love him, don't you?" Clay's eyes searched hers, reading the answer even before she spoke.

"Yes." The one word was all she could get out without risking tears.

"Oh, half-pint." He sighed, his face twisting in sympathy and Angie felt tears flood her eyes, overflowing before she could force them back.

"Damn." She dabbed at the tears with the end of her robe's belt, a completely inadequate hankie. "Damn, damn, damn. Thank you," she muttered when Clay handed her a paper towel. "I wasn't going to cry anymore. He's not worth it. I *know* he's not worth it. I don't know why I still care."

"But you do," he said, finishing for her.

"Yes." She sniffed back a new flood of tears and scrubbed her cheeks with the rough towel. "But what he's doing is wrong. I couldn't just let him get away with it, no matter how I feel about him."

Clay frowned, looked about to say something and then changed his mind. Getting up, he went to get the coffeepot. Bringing it back, he filled both their cups before setting the pot on the tile insert in the middle of the island.

"Did you get any sleep at all last night?" he asked.

"Some." Angie shrugged, unconcerned with her lack of sleep. "Are you going to arrest him? Do you need more evidence?"

"I don't need more evidence," he said absently, staring at his coffee.

"Will I . . . will I have to testify against him?" Her imagination couldn't even encompass that thought.

"No. The truth is, there's more to this than you know," he said slowly, seeming to come to some decision.

"What do you mean? You didn't know about Travis, did you? You couldn't have," she said, answering her own question. "You would have said something to me if you'd known what he was doing."

"Morgan didn't try to defend himself?" he asked. "He didn't say anything at all about there maybe being more to the story than what you saw?"

"No." Angie shook her head, trying to figure out where this conversation was going. Maybe it was lack of sleep that was making it so hard to follow. "What are you getting at? Do you know something about Travis?''

"I pulled his file," he said slowly. "I was looking for something on him, something concrete enough to make you stay away from him."

"Then you *knew* about this? You knew he was selling drugs and you didn't say anything to me?" She stared at him in hurt disbelief.

"That's not what I found in his file." The reluctance in his tone made Angie suspect that there was something even worse in the file, though what could be worse than selling drugs, she couldn't imagine.

"What was in there?" Even as she asked the question, she didn't want to hear the answer. She didn't want to know what Clay had found. Didn't want to hear what Travis had done. She wanted to throw her hands over her ears and close her eyes to shut out whatever Clay had to tell her. Instead, she sat there, staring at her brother's face with eyes that begged him to spare her any more blows.

"I shouldn't say anything," he said slowly. "But I probably shouldn't have been digging through the files in the first place."

"What has he done?" There was a kind of despairing resignation in her tone.

"He's not a drug dealer, Angie." The bald statement glanced off the protective wall she'd thrown up. She stared at him without comprehension.

"He's not selling drugs," Clay said, more forcefully. "What you heard—it wasn't what it seemed."

"I heard him making a deal. He didn't deny it." Hadn't he understood what she'd told him?

"He didn't deny it because it would have blown his cover," Clay said.

"His cover?" Angie stared at him as the meaning of those two words slowly sank in. "His cover?"

"He's on our side." It was obvious that Clay didn't particularly like admitting as much.

"His cover?" Her voice had risen. "He's a cop?"

"He's working with the police," Clay corrected. "It's an unusual setup."

"He's not dealing drugs?" She had to hear him say it again before she dared to allow even the smallest ray of hope to penetrate the black cloud of despair. "You're sure?"

"He's not dealing drugs," Clay said, his tone definite. "He's working with us. Apparently he contacted the people we had watching Shearson and offered to use his old connection to Shearson to penetrate the organization and bring Shearson down."

"Travis used to work for a drug dealer?" Angie rubbed her fingers over her forehead, trying to still her spinning thoughts. She didn't know whether she should be feeling relieved, or angry, or hurt. All three emotions were tangled up inside her.

"When he lived in Salem before. I told you he was in trouble then," he reminded her. "There was never enough evidence to arrest him but there was never any doubt about what he was up to. Shearson was into stealing cars then and Morgan was part of the ring. He was good enough to avoid getting caught."

"He stole cars?" Angie could hear the dazed note in her voice but she couldn't seem to grasp what he was telling her. First, Clay told her that Travis wasn't a drug dealer and before she'd had a chance to feel relieved about that, he was telling her that he was a car thief.

"There was no proof," he admitted. "About ten years ago, he quit Shearson's organization and left town. That was the last I heard of him until he showed up again. Apparently, when he offered to help the police, his connections were just too good to pass up."

"So he's not dealing drugs. He's working *with* the police to try to catch this Shearson?" She wanted everything to be stated very clearly, with no room for misunderstanding.

"That's right. But that doesn't make him Dudley Do-Right, either," he cautioned. "Morgan's past is checkered, to say the least. I only told you this because I didn't want you to think that you were going to have to testify against the guy. I still don't want you having anything to do with him."

But he was talking to himself. Angie was no longer listening. Travis wasn't selling drugs. And she wasn't going to have to watch them send him to prison. Everything was going to be all right, after all.

"I'm going to kill him," she announced, interrupting Clay's mutterings about her staying away from Travis.

"What, now that you know he's one of the good guys, you're going to kill him?" He looked at her, puzzled by this line of thinking.

"He should have told me."

"No, he shouldn't have. *I* shouldn't have told you now. There's only a handful of people in this town who know about it, Angie."

"Well, I should have been one of them," she said stubbornly. "He shouldn't have let me leave, thinking what I thought."

"He did exactly what he had to." It was obvious that Clay didn't like making that admission but fairness dictated it.

"I told him I loved him, Clay. I told him I loved him and he still didn't say a word." Her tone was a mixture of hurt and anger.

"What did he say when you told him how you felt?" Clay struggled to keep his tone neutral.

"Nothing. I told him I loved him but that I couldn't accept what he was doing. And he just said he understood and let me leave."

"Angie, I don't want to argue his side—you know I don't want you involved with him—but it *is* part of his job not to tell people, even people he cares about, who he is. And he may have been trying to protect you,'' he added reluctantly.

''From what?''

''From what he's involved in. *Travis* may not be a drug dealer but the people he's trying to bring down are. This may have seemed the best way to keep you safe.'' The fact that the words were spoken somewhat grudgingly gave them more impact.

Angie nibbled on her lower lip, considering what he'd said. Yes, Travis would have let her believe he was a drug dealer if he thought it would keep her safe. How many times had he insisted that Clay was right to tell her to stay away from him? For some reason, he was convinced he was no good for her. Maybe this had been the perfect opportunity to keep her away from him, for her own good, of course.

''I'm not a child,'' she said, annoyed by this additional proof of male stupidity. ''I don't want or need the two of you deciding what's best for me.''

''Angie—''

''No.'' She cut him off with a sharp gesture of her hand. ''I mean it, Clay. You've got to stop treating me like I'm still ten years old. No more warning me about Travis and no more extracting promises from him that he'll keep me safe.''

''I've been taking care of you a long time. It's a hard habit to break.''

"I know." Angie leaned toward him, putting her hand on his arm, her eyes full of love. "But I can take care of myself now."

Clay looked at her, forcing himself to see, not the child she'd been, but the woman she'd become. He felt a pang of regret. She wasn't his baby sister anymore. And she was right to demand that he treat her as an adult, capable of making her own decisions.

"You won't mind if I worry about you, will you? I'm not sure I can break that habit."

"Worry all you want but keep your mouth shut." Her smile softened the harshness of her words and Clay laughed.

"Now, all I have to do is convince Travis not to be an idiot," she said, sitting up straight on the stool.

"Stay away from Travis." Clay's tone made the words an order and Angie's head jerked toward him in disbelief.

"I thought we just settled this," she said.

"I'm not talking as your brother now, Angie. I'm talking as a police officer. Stay away from Travis."

"But he thinks I hate him," she protested.

"You can explain later. Right now, I don't want you anywhere near him, for his sake as well as yours," he added when she opened her mouth to argue. "If he cares about you, you're a distraction he can't afford."

Angie argued but Clay forced her to admit the logic in what he was saying. If Travis had to worry about her safety as well as his own it could prove fatal.

The word "fatal" was distressing. All Clay's assurances that Travis had all the protection the police could offer were scant comfort. Nor could he tell her how long it might be before the case was brought to a conclusion and she'd be able to see Travis.

By the time he announced that he had to leave for work, Angie's head was starting to spin. Too much had happened in too short a space of time. She'd plunged lower than she'd ever been in her life. And then Clay had told her that she wasn't in love with a drug dealer, after all, and she'd felt her spirits skyrocket.

Yet she couldn't have what she wanted most of all, which was to see Travis and make things right between them. It was just a matter of time, she told herself. Patience. She just had to be patient and everything would work out right.

PATIENCE, Travis told himself. Patience was a major requirement for a job like this. He had a meeting with Shearson in a little less than six hours. Shearson had reacted exactly as he'd expected, taking the bait as neatly as a trout swallowing a fly. His police department contact hadn't been happy about the way he'd pushed the meeting. Travis suspected that his annoyance was caused by the fact that Travis had accom-

plished in a few weeks what the police had been trying
to do for several years.

Of course, he hadn't accomplished anything yet. If
there was one thing he knew about Shearson, it was
that the man was unpredictable. Shearson claimed he
was ready to buy the drugs, but he could just as easily
be setting him up for a nasty fall. There'd been something in Sinclair's tone when he called to set up the
meeting that made Travis uneasy.

But there was nothing to do now but go to the ap-
pointed place and see what happened. And until then,
all he could do was wait. Wait and think.

He stared up at the dark ceiling and wished he hadn't
quit smoking five years ago. A cigarette would give him
something to do right about now.

Sixteen hours since Angie had walked out. He didn't
need to close his eyes to remember the way she'd looked
at him, the pain in her eyes. She'd been devastated by
what she thought she'd discovered. And she'd still said
she loved him. Hated him, too, from the look in her
eyes, but he couldn't blame her for that.

Travis put his hands under his head, and listened to
the rattle of the fan that he'd moved from the living
room into the bedroom with the vague hope that it
would make it easier to sleep. From the sound of the
motor, it wasn't going to last much longer. But then, if
things worked out the way he hoped, he wasn't going
to need it much longer, anyway.

He wanted this mess with Shearson settled. He wanted to get on with his life and get everything out in the open. He wanted a chance to tell Angie the truth.

A guilty conscience had driven him to approach the police. He'd offered his connections with Shearson, his knowledge of the man, as a way to atone for past sins. He certainly hadn't been expecting to fall in love. But fall in love he had, with a pair of big blue eyes and a soft smile. A cop's sister. If it hadn't been so damned tragic, it might have been funny.

If Shearson took the bait, the whole mess could be wrapped up in a matter of days. His life would be his again, the way it had been before he'd been overtaken by this sudden urge to play Good Samaritan.

He'd be able to leave this house to its gentle decline. He'd get a motel room somewhere in town and spend his time convincing Angie to forgive him. If she'd give him another chance, he'd do his damnedest to court her the way she deserved.

His mouth curved in a smile. Courting her. Yeah, he liked the sound of that. He might have been a little slow-witted about figuring it out but he'd finally realized that he loved her. And he wasn't going to walk out of her life without at least trying to put things right again.

She'd said she loved him and his angel wasn't a woman who loved lightly. Once he had a chance to explain things to her, to make her understand, she'd forgive him for not telling her the truth—at least he hoped that's what would happen.

His smile faded and was replaced by an uneasy frown. She had to forgive him. He'd waited a long time to fall in love. He wasn't going to give up on her—on them—without a fight.

Chapter Thirteen

Angie arched her back to ease the ache that had settled between her shoulders. She didn't know whether to be glad or sorry that her shift was up. She'd had almost no sleep but she didn't feel particularly tired. The events of last night and this morning made mundane concerns such as sleep unimportant.

It had been a relatively slow day at the clinic, giving Angie more time to think than she'd really wanted. Her thoughts careened back and forth, from how much she loved Travis to the way he'd let her think the worst of him. Her emotions had been no more stable than her thoughts, spinning from relief to anger without ever settling on one or the other.

She was exhausted, physically and emotionally. She wanted—needed—to see Travis, to talk to him, to try to understand what had happened, why he'd lied to her. But Clay had done a good job of convincing her that she had to keep her distance from Travis, for his sake as well as her own.

Sighing, she picked up her purse and scrambled in the bottom of it for her car keys. She tried not to think about the danger Travis might be in. She didn't need Clay to tell her that he was playing a very dangerous game. If this Shearson found out... Shivering, she closed the thought out of her mind. She had to believe that Travis knew what he was doing, that he wouldn't take any unnecessary chances. And that he'd come out safe in the end.

So she could strangle him.

"See you tomorrow, Angie." Janine lifted a hand from her typewriter to wave.

"Bye, Janine." Angie returned the wave and pushed open the door. The heat rolled over her, nearly stealing her breath. *It must be ninety-five in the shade,* she thought, lifting one hand to shield her eyes as they adjusted to the bright sunshine.

Travis's house would be baking with nothing but that inadequate fan to cool it. Not that she'd minded the heat, she admitted. They'd generated enough heat between them to make the temperature unimportant.

She wasn't going to think about that now. She didn't want to think of anything to do with Travis. Not now. Not until she'd gained a little distance from the situation and could try to figure out just what it was she felt.

"Miss Brady?" Angie was nearly to her car when she heard the hesitant call. She turned, narrowing her eyes against the sun.

A slight figure hovered near one of the shrubs that marched along the edge of the parking lot, hanging back in their shadows.

"Tony?" She moved closer, confirming her guess as to his identity. Tony Aggretti. She hadn't seen much of him since that momentous day when Travis had come to her rescue. "Hello."

"Hi." He returned her smile with a nervous grimace, his eyes darting uneasily from one side to the other.

"How's your mother?" Angie asked, wondering at the boy's obvious uneasiness. She'd only seen him once since the incident with Billy Sikes and that had been at a distance. She noticed that he'd lost weight and wondered if he was getting enough to eat.

"She's okay." He lifted his thin shoulders in a quick shrug. "You friends with that guy? The one with the bike?"

"Travis?" Angie felt all her senses snap to attention. "Yes, we're friends. Why?"

Tony shrugged again, his eyes never quite settling in one place. He looked as if he regretted having approached her, but now that Travis's name had come up, Angie had no intention of letting him go without learning what he had to say.

"What did you want to tell me, Tony?" She forced her voice to calm authority when what she really wanted to do was grab him and shake whatever it was out of him.

"He gave my mom some money," he said. "And you've been good to us. If it wasn't for the clinic, a lot of people wouldn't make it around here. Mom says you're an angel."

The compliment brought a sharp pang, reminding her of Travis. She forced a smile.

"I wouldn't go that far. What did you want to tell me, Tony?"

"That guy? The one with the bike?" She nodded and then had to tamp down the urge to scream when he hesitated yet again. Just when she was sure she was going to have to shake the information out of him, he started talking, the words tumbling over themselves as if he was afraid to slow down.

"I heard them talking and he's walkin' into a trap."

"You heard who talking?"

"I can't tell you." He gave her a pleading look. "They'd kill me if they found out I talked to you, Miss Brady."

"Okay. Just tell me what you can." Angie's nails dug holes into the leather of her purse but not a trace of urgency showed in her voice.

"Billy and me, we was…was pickin' up some stuff." From the way he hesitated, his eyes avoiding hers,

Angie had a pretty good idea what the "stuff" was but now was not the time to pursue the issue.

"Go on."

"I overheard them talking about that guy. They said they told him he'd be meeting the boss but that the boss was out of the country and they were just going to take the stuff he was bringing and kill him. I think they're planning on selling it on the side and not tell their boss at all," he said shrewdly, showing an appalling knowledge of human nature for one so young.

"Where is this meeting supposed to take place, Tony? And when? Do you know when?"

"I think it's today sometime but I don't know where it is. That's the truth, Miss Brady. I told you all I know."

"That's okay. You did the right thing, Tony." She had to get to Travis, had to warn him. The rules had suddenly changed and Clay's edict had no meaning in this situation. On the other hand, maybe Clay would have a better chance of finding him in time. Yes, that was best. She'd go to Clay.

She was unaware of having spoken the thought out loud until a new voice entered the conversation.

"I don't think so, Nurse Brady." The last words were spoken with mocking emphasis that was familiar. Billy Sikes. She'd recognize that smirking tone anywhere. She started to turn to face him but the move was never completed.

"Don't!" She heard Tony's cry but there was no time to react to the warning. There was a sharp pain behind her ear and she felt her knees give way as she sank into a whirling blackness.

Her last conscious thought was that this couldn't be happening in broad daylight. And then she didn't think anything at all.

TRAVIS APPROACHED the warehouse cautiously. When Sinclair had called to say that Shearson had agreed to the meeting, Travis had had the sudden, uneasy feeling that this was going too well. Maybe he'd been too clever for his own good. But he couldn't back out now.

So he'd agreed to the meeting and gotten in touch with his contact to arrange for backup. If Shearson really did show up and they could get something on film, they might be able to nail him immediately. Getting anything on film was not going to be easy. The warehouse was in an industrial district and provided few hiding places, which was no doubt exactly why it had been chosen.

His contact had promised to have men in place. With shotgun mikes and telephoto lenses and some luck, maybe they'd get something that could be used in court. It was the luck part of it that made Travis uneasy. He'd never trusted things that depended on luck.

The warehouse looked peaceful enough, he thought. In fact, when he cut the bike's engine, the silence was practically deafening. It was a Saturday afternoon and the area was deserted. So there'd be no witnesses? he wondered.

He swung his leg over the bike and reached up to lift his helmet off, his eyes skimming the area. There was no sign of the men he'd been promised would be in position. But then, if he'd been able to see them, they wouldn't have been doing a very good job.

Setting the helmet on the bike's seat, he thrust his fingers through his hair. He needed a haircut, he thought absently, still taking stock of the area. He flexed his shoulders and resisted the urge to check the gun tucked in the small of his back. They'd be expecting him to be armed. After all, they weren't in a particularly trusting business.

He unstrapped the black briefcase from the back of the bike and walked around to the side door, as instructed. He knocked. There was only a brief wait before it was opened. Travis didn't recognize the man who opened it but he recognized the type—hired muscle, to use a phrase from an earlier era. Dangerous enough but fairly predictable. He'd do what he was told but he wasn't likely to make any rash decisions on his own.

Travis nodded and walked past, wishing he knew just what the guy had been told. It would be helpful if he knew the day's agenda, especially whether it contained any plans for bumping off upstart suppliers.

Sinclair and Drasen were waiting for him in the center of the warehouse but there was no sign of Shearson. The building was mostly empty, although there were a few crates stacked against the wall. A white limo was parked in the center of the huge room. Sinclair leaned against the hood while Drasen stood nearby. Both turned toward him as he stepped into sight.

"Good afternoon." Sinclair's greeting was impeccably polite, his smile socially correct.

"Good afternoon." Travis grinned, letting his amusement show. He could almost come to like Sinclair, he thought. The man was an original.

"You brought what we agreed on?" Sinclair asked.

"It's here." Travis lifted the briefcase, which contained cocaine borrowed from the police evidence room. The street value was enough to allow a man to retire for life. "Where's Shearson?" He eyed the tinted windows on the limousine.

"We have the money. But before we make the exchange, we'd like to examine the merchandise. It's not that we don't trust you. It's just good business."

"Of course." Travis didn't miss the way Sinclair had avoided his question about Shearson. Nor was he unaware of the fact that he was neatly caught between the two of them in front and the goon behind him. The hair on the back of his neck was starting to stand up.

He moved forward slowly, looking for a way out of a situation that suddenly seemed most unhealthy.

"Where's Shearson? I already told you I don't deal with middlemen."

"Yes, so you said. Unfortunately Mr. Shearson was unable to attend this meeting." Sinclair shrugged apologetically. "But knowing of your aversion to dealing with—what was it you said?—ah yes, flunkies, Mr. Drasen and I have decided to oblige you by going into business for ourselves."

"Double-crossing Shearson?" Travis grinned, his fingers tightening over the briefcase. "Pretty dangerous, isn't it?"

"I don't think the late Mr. Shearson will object too strenuously."

"The *late* Mr. Shearson?" Travis questioned sharply.

"Yes. We received word late last evening. He met with an accident while on his yacht. Most unfortunate."

And not only for Shearson, Travis thought. He was surprised to feel a pang of real regret at the thought that Shearson was dead. He couldn't say he'd ever liked the man and he certainly hadn't trusted him but, in the old days, he'd known him intimately enough to see the humanity behind the amoral facade.

But there was no time for regrets now. He had the distinct feeling that another "unfortunate accident" was in his own near future, if Sinclair had his way.

"Well, I don't care what happened to Shearson," he said, shrugging to show his indifference. "I'll deal with whoever is in charge."

"How gracious of you, Mr. Morgan." Travis had once seen a piranha with a very similar smile. "Perhaps if we could see your merchandise?"

"Sure." Travis started forward only to come to a halt as the sounds of a scuffle came from the right and a little behind him. From the quick frown that marred Sinclair's smooth features, it was clear that this hadn't been in his plans. And anything not in Sinclair's plans might be a good thing for him.

He turned his head just as a familiar figure stumbled out from between two crates.

"Angel!" The exclamation escaped him as he took a quick step toward her.

"It's a trap, Travis," she shouted as soon as she saw him. "They're going to kill you."

There was a moment of frozen silence and then it seemed as if all hell broke loose. Travis saw Billy Sikes lunge behind Angie, grabbing for her. Out the corner of his eye, he saw Drasen's hand disappear inside his coat. And then his fingers were closing over his own gun.

He fired and saw Drasen jerk with the impact of the bullet. He fired again and then stumbled back, the breath driven from him as Sinclair's bullet slammed into him. The bulletproof vest he wore under his shirt prevented penetration but it didn't do anything to lessen the impact of the slug.

And then it seemed as if it was hailing bullets. *The cavalry,* he thought whimsically. He shoved himself away from the crate he'd fallen against and threw himself toward Angie who, he noted in some surprise, had just laid out Billy Sikes with a very nice right to the jaw.

He felt the air whoosh out of her as he slammed into her, taking her to the cement floor in a rolling dive that brought them to a halt between two crates. And there they stayed frozen, Travis's body covering hers protectively.

It seemed as if the shooting went on for hours but Travis knew it could only have been a matter of a minute or two, at most. The silence returned as abruptly as it had disappeared. He lifted his head slowly, peering out at the slice of warehouse visible to him.

Billy Sikes lay sprawled on the floor, unconscious but apparently unwounded. He couldn't see Drasen but he knew he was dead—he'd seen where his bullets hit. He could see Sinclair's leg, easily recognizable by the pale gray suit he'd been wearing. *A natty dresser, Sinclair,* he thought, apropos of nothing. Or he had been. Something about the angle of that leg suggested that Sinclair wasn't going to have much use for a wardrobe anymore.

Assured that the good guys had won this one, he sat up, drawing Angie up with him.

"Are you hurt?" he asked, brushing the hair back from her face.

For answer, she drew back her fist and aimed a furious blow at his chin. Travis jerked back to avoid the blow, smacking the back of his head against the wooden crate behind him as her fist skimmed past his face.

"Damn you!" Her voice was shaking with anger. She aimed another punch. "Damn you!"

This time, he caught her hand in his, closing his fingers around her fist, his other arm sweeping around her back to pull her close.

"I'm sorry." He didn't waste time asking why she was cursing him. "I couldn't tell you."

"You let me think you were selling drugs." She got the words out, trying to push herself away from him.

"I had to. I was afraid you were going to get hurt." Travis refused to release her. If he let her go, he might never get her back again. He had to hold her, make her understand. "I was going to tell you the truth when it was over."

"Hah." The single disgusted syllable was all she had the breath for. He was holding her so close, she could hardly breathe. But he was alive and safe and holding onto her as if he'd never let her go.

She closed her eyes for a moment, the fingers of her free hand curling into the fabric of his shirt, feeling the stiffness of the body armor beneath.

"When I saw him shoot you—" She shuddered, remembering that instant. She'd never forget seeing the bullet strike him, sending him back against the packing crates. She'd felt a panicked rage she'd never known before, felt the adrenaline surge through her. "I hurt my hand punching Billy Sikes," she said suddenly.

"You knocked him out cold." Travis had released her fist and was running his fingers over her hair. "How did you get here? I nearly died when I saw you."

She felt a faint tremor in his hand and knew that the sight of her had shaken him as badly as seeing him shot had shaken her. Somewhere beyond the narrow alleyway that held them, she could hear people stirring around. Once or twice, someone called Travis's name but he didn't seem to notice and she was in no mood to point it out to him.

"Tony Aggretti came to tell me that you were walking into a trap. I was going to get Clay, but Billy knocked me out."

"I'll wring his neck." Travis's fingers found the knot behind her ear, exploring it with gentle fingers.

"Not if I wring yours first." She wasn't quite ready to give up her anger.

She leaned back, tilting her head until she could see his face. "Why didn't you tell me the truth last night?"

"I couldn't, Angel." His eyes asked her to understand. "I'd already put you in danger just by getting involved with you. Your brother was right about that— I had no business putting you in the line of fire. I knew it from the start."

"Then why did you?"

Travis hesitated, his fingers tangled in her hair, his eyes uncertain. "I couldn't seem to stay away," he admitted finally. "I kept telling myself I was going to and then I'd find some excuse to see you again."

"Why?"

She could see the answer in his eyes but she'd just spent the most miserable twenty-four hours of her life and she wasn't going to let him off the hook quite so easily. She wanted to hear him say the words, and then she'd decide whether to smack him or kiss him.

"I love you." He gave her the words without hesitation, gave her his heart without reservation. And Angie felt all the anger drain out of her.

"I should make you suffer," she whispered. But her fingers had found the hole in his shirt and she could feel the bullet buried in the vest he wore. She'd come so close to losing him, had thought she'd seen him killed right in front of her. There were still questions to be answered—some of them important.

But nothing was as important as the fact that he was here, holding her. And he was safe.

CLAY BRADY stopped and stared at the couple embracing between the packing boxes. They didn't seem to notice that they were sitting on cold, hard cement. Obviously neither of them had heard him calling Angie's name. His heart had nearly stopped when one of the officers had told him that she'd been there during the shooting.

But she didn't seem any the worse for the wear. In fact, judging by the way her arms were linked around Morgan's neck, she was in pretty good shape. He hesitated and then turned away without disturbing them. There'd be time enough for explanations later.

"I LOVE YOU, TOO," Angie said finally, oblivious to her brother's departure. "But don't think I'm going to forgive you that easily. I'm going to make you pay for scaring me, for letting me think that you were selling drugs."

"I may not have sold drugs but I've done things you wouldn't like." The look in Travis's eyes said he was determined that there be no more lies between them.

"It doesn't matter." Angie lifted her hand to brush a lock of dark blond hair back from his forehead. "I love you. And you love me. Nothing else matters as much as that."

Travis pulled her closer, his mouth closing over hers in affirmation. He didn't care what was going on beyond this narrow little aisle between the crates. He didn't care about anything but the woman in his arms.

Angie loved him. Despite everything he'd been, everything that had happened, she loved him. She was right. Nothing mattered beyond that.

COMING NEXT MONTH

THAT SAME OLD FEELING Judith Duncan

Wide Open Spaces

Chase McCall was coming home; his path led him straight to the only woman he'd ever really loved. Would she believe he could stay for good this time and give him just one more chance?

DEFENDER Kathleen Eagle

Gideon Defender had let Raina go once in the name of love and she'd married another. Now she was a widow bringing her adopted son home to embrace his Indian culture and Gideon knew his secret child might need him. What was Raina's reaction going to be?

NIGHT OF THE JAGUAR Merline Lovelace

Code Name: Danger

Jake MacKenzie had a dangerous assignment before Sarah Chandler and the children she was looking after came along. They made it doubly difficult. How was he going to keep his hands off his 'prisoner' day after day, night after steaming night?

MACDOUGALL'S DARLING Emilie Richards

The Men of Midnight

Andrew MacDougall made Fiona Sinclair ready to face her future— she now wanted a real home, a family, a husband by her side. But although Andrew would do many things to protect his home and his woman, he would never marry…

AND A MYSTERY GIFT

FREE

Return this coupon and we'll send you 4 Silhouette Sensation novels and a mystery gift absolutely FREE! We'll even pay the postage and packing for you.

We're making you this offer to introduce you to the benefits of Reader Service: FREE home delivery of brand-new Silhouette novels, at least a month before they are available in the shops, FREE gifts and a monthly Newsletter packed with information.

Accepting these FREE books and gift places you under no obligation to buy, you may cancel at any time, even after receiving just your free shipment. Simply complete the coupon below and send it to:

SILHOUETTE READER SERVICE, FREEPOST, CROYDON, CR9 3WZ.

No stamp needed

Yes, please send me 4 free Silhouette Sensation novels and a mystery gift. I understand that unless you hear from me, I will receive 4 superb new titles every month for just £2.30* each postage and packing free. I am under no obligation to purchase any books and I may cancel or suspend my subscription at any time, but the free books and gifts will be mine to keep in any case. (I am over 18 years of age)

1EP6SS

Ms/Mrs/Miss/Mr _____

Address _____

_____

_____ Postcode _____

Offer closes 31st December 1996. We reserve the right to refuse an application. *Prices and terms subject to change without notice. Offer only valid in UK and Ireland and is not available to current subscribers to this series. **Readers in Ireland please write to: P.O. Box 4546, Dublin 24.** Overseas readers please write for details.

You may be mailed with offers from other reputable companies as a result of this application. Please tick box if you would prefer not to receive such offers.

COMING NEXT MONTH FROM
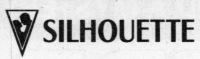 SILHOUETTE

Intrigue
Danger, deception and desire

TOUCH A WILD HEART Vella Munn
ON THE SCENT M.J. Rodgers
IMMINENT THUNDER Rachel Lee
LETHAL LOVER Laura Gordon

Special Edition
Satisfying romances packed with emotion

DADDY TO THE RESCUE Cathy Gillen Thacker
**THE MAN, THE MOON AND THE
MARRIAGE VOW** Christine Rimmer
FRIENDS, LOVERS...AND BABIES! Joan Elliott Pickart
BUCHANAN'S BRIDE Pamela Toth
CHILD OF MIDNIGHT Sharon De Vita
THE WEDDING CONTRACT Kelly Jamison

Desire
*Provocative, sensual love stories for the
woman of today*

MEGAN'S MARRIAGE Annette Broadrick
ASSIGNMENT: MARRIAGE Jackie Merritt
REESE: THE UNTAMED Susan Connell
THIS IS MY CHILD Lucy Gordon
TYLER Diana Palmer
HUSBAND MATERIAL Rita Rainville